Wolf Song

Wolf Song
Harvey Fergusson

UNIVERSITY OF NEBRASKA PRESS
LINCOLN and LONDON

First Bison Book printing: 1981
Most recent printing indicated by first digit below:
3   4   5   6   7   8   9   10

Library of Congress Cataloging in Publication Data

Fergusson, Harvey, 1890–1971.
  Wolf song.

  I. Title.
[PS3511.E55W64 1981]   813'.52   81–3056
ISBN 0–8032–6855–6 (pbk.)
AACR2

Reprinted by arrangement with William Morrow & Co., Inc.

∞

Wolf Song

For Rebecca

CHAPTER ONE

I

P from the edge of the prairie and over the range rode three. Their buckskin was black with blood and shiny from much wiping of greasy knives and nearly all the fringes had been cut off their pants for thongs. Hair hung thick and dirty to their shoulders. Traps rattled in rucksacks behind their Spanish saddles and across the pommel each carried a long Hawkins rifle of shining brass-bound steel and battered wooden stock. Six pack mules bulged with square bales of beaver worth eight dollars a pound in St. Louis and six in the mountains.

They travelled in a long string, old Rube Thatcher leading and Gullion and young Sam Lash hard at the rumps of the mules, cursing any that straggled. All of their stock was gaunt from long going but still they rode hard with iron spurs ajingle against their horses' ribs.

More wealth was in their packs than any of

them had seen before and the old town of Taos was just the other side of the range.

White liquor and brown women, fat eating and store fixings lay before them and a year of hard days lay behind.

"Hump yourself, you goddam mule! This chile's half froze for liquor!"

White corn liquor for a man that's been half froze all winter.

Brown willing women for a man that ain't seen a skirt since last spring.

Round loaves of white bread, brown beans and red chile for a man that's lived on wild meat for a year.

"Hump yourself, you goddam mule! This outfit's bound for Taos!"

2

They had trapped up the South Platte in the fall when cottonwood was yellow in the bottoms and cold winds blew swarming wildfowl out of the north and early snow tipped blue mountains white. All day long they worked waist deep in cold muddy water, setting traps and tending traps with a careful patient art and one eye on the bushes where Ute and Rapaho might hide. While light lasted they skinned beaver and stretched pelts on willow frames and fleshed and grained and baled them. By firelight they boiled and roasted meat and ate it in chunks unsalted with strips of buffalo fat for bread. Then they mended moccasins and moulded bullets and cursed the weather and the Indians. After fourteen hours' hard work two slept and one watched, listening for the snort of a mule that would mean the smell of brown skin in the bushes.

It was a hell of a life and they often said they'd quit it, but no one ever did. You never quit the mountains till you got rubbed out.

Utes sneaked in one black stormy night, crawling on all fours, dressed in wolf skins, snap-snapping buffalo bones to sound like coyotes. They jumped up with a whoop and stampeded all the stock. Old Rube Thatcher up and knocked one cold but the rest got away with the cavvayard.

They cached their packs and took the Indian trail and hung to it mad and hungry three days and nights. They slept cold and chewed jerked meat and said little. Old Rube Thatcher had a picture of the country in his head and he saw the Utes were heading for the Middle Park. So they left the trail on the flats and climbed the range and killed two elk and ate raw liver and slept under wet hides. Next day they crawled up on the Indian village and shot right into a war

[3]

dance and the way those Utes streaked it would take the gristle off a painter's tail. They lifted hair off three and got back all their mules but one the Indians ate, and three Ute ponies paid for that. So they went back to work after five days lost.

They trapped that fall from the lower flats where beaver lived in bank holes and cut cottonwood to near timber-line where beaver dammed streams a foot wide and built big lodges and cut quaking asp. Everywhere beaver were thick and fur was heavy. When snow came they forted up in South Park where short thick grass curls and cures on a flat fifteen miles wide with sheltering mountains all around. They built a cottonwood corral for the stock and a log shanty with a dirt roof and stone fireplace for themselves. When buffalo began to drift in for the winter they made meat and hung it on frames to dry and scraped robes for winter beds and then holed up to wait for spring.

Snow fell deep and there was nothing to do but cut wood and smoke and swap lies. Young Sam Lash was an upancoming liar but he couldn't shine with old Rube. Rube had been everywhere when everything happened. Sam figured he was at least a hundred and fifty to have been everywhere he'd been and done everything he'd done. Old Rube admitted that when he came to the mountains Pike's Peak was a hole in the ground. He was at Salt Lake the year of the big storm when it snowed for seventy days and the snow was seventy feet deep. Whole herds of buffalo were frozen, he said, and in the spring they dug them up, fresh as a new-laid egg, and threw them into the lake and had pickled humps enough to last the Ute nation a hundred years.

He told about the white giants with red hair and green eyes that lived on an island in Salt Lake and rode on hairy elephants. Nobody had ever seen them but old Rube had seen logs drift in that were big as a hogshead and had been cut with axes four feet wide.

Rube was one more coon that had been to the famous petrified country. The way he told it he was going through a desert and had starved four days when he came to a country where grass was green and flowers blooming and birds singing and he sang out "Hurrah for summer doins." He up and cracked at a bird in a tree and it flew into a thousand pieces and when the mules bit the grass it splintered and cut their mouths. Everything was petrified, even the water in the streams, and the gooseberries along the creek were emeralds and the raspberries were rubies. He gathered him a rucksack full of jewelry and pulled out of there but he had to empty the sack to save weight before he made the next water and all he brought away was one ruby. He showed them that. Gullion said it wasn't any ruby but just a garnet, like you could get off any Navajo, and the other two gave Gullion the laugh. He was simple as a kit beaver.

Lash twitted Rube about the Boiling Spring on the head of the Arkansas that was the biggest kind of medicine because a devil lived in it who could change a man's luck. Everybody knew Rube went there every year and smoked a pipe of kinnik-kinnik and blew smoke to the four quarters and made a prayer he had learned off a Crow medicine man. He believed that was the only reason he still had his hair and made beaver every year. He told how Black Harris went there once and said he didn't believe in any Indian devil and spit in the spring. The devil came out and grappled him and they wrastled all night and finally Black Harris threw the devil back in. After that his luck was so good beaver used to come up on the bank and run after him to be skinned.

Along in January it snowed so deep the horses couldn't reach grass even on the windswept flats and they had to cut cottonwood trees and use the top twigs for fodder and even then one mule died. It was so cold and the wind blew so hard a man could only work about fifteen minutes at a stretch.

They took turns cutting fodder and firewood all day long and they were never warm. Huddled in together they began to hate each other a little as men in winter quarters always will. When Sam Lash told that his mother's family in Virginia had owned niggers and a Concord coach, Gullion got mad. He said if Sam Lash thought he could shine in the mountains because his folks owned niggers back in the States he was plumb loco. He said in the mountains a man was on his own and where he came from was nobody's business.

Gullion was a hard case. Both his ears were clipped off across the top. He claimed they had been bitten off in a ruction at Taos but anyone could see they were cut clean and some knew they cut the ears off convicts in the state of Delaware. Gullion was a good trapper and scared of nothing but when he got fight in him he was bad. When Lash told him to go to hell he began to slobber and his hands began to work and he said he'd bitten the nose off a man for telling him to go to hell once and he was half froze for a ruction anyway. Lash stood up and told him to come on but old Rube got between. He said if Gullion felt like chawing noses he could go out and try to chaw the nose off a Ute. He said this was no time for social doings and if those two wanted to fight they could wait till they hit Taos. He got him a

[7]

big stick of cottonwood and told them the minute they tangled he'd crack the man that started it right behind the ears. So then they shut up.

Rube got down on his luck too and said a man was a fool to spend his life in the mountains. He said he felt like pulling for Missouri to trap a squaw and settle down and eat Johnny cake and hominy the rest of his life.

He said that every year but of course he never went. No man ever left buffalo hump to eat hog. You never quit the mountains till you got rubbed out.

When water began to run in late March they pulled for the flats of the South Platte and started to trap again, working into high country as the weather opened and geese went yelping north and beaver came out of their lodges to wet their slides and cut timber. By the time the cottonwoods showed green and buffalo calves dropped they had beaver packs as heavy as ever three men took out of the mountains and there was nothing for it but to hit the Taos trail.

3

"Hump yourself, you goddam mule! Beaver buys liquor and this chile's got a dry!"

On the eastern slope snow still lay deep under

heavy spruce timber and they floundered upward slow and hard, but where they came out on top of the divide above timber-line new grass was already up in the sun, wild sheep ran for the rocky peaks, marmots whistled and ptarmigan whirred. They stopped to blow their horses and looked east across a hundred miles of prairie and west to the white broken tops of the San Juan range fifty miles away. Down on the flat country dark living masses seemed to move.

"I can see buffalo travelling," says Sam Lash, shading his eyes. He claimed to be able to see farther than any man he ever met. Old Rube shaded his eyes and looked too.

"Yessir," he said. "Damned if it ain't, and one old bull's got a flea on his hump!"

"I cain't see nothin'," Gullion said, "but old Taos and this child bellyin' up to a bar. Step out, you goddam mule! Cain't you smell that licker?"

"Is that all you can see?" says Rube while they rode.

"Nossir! I can see a Mexican gal I know, and boy she's some punkin! She can dance like a Ute that's counted coup."

"Is that all she can do?" says Rube, while they loped.

"Nossir! She can cook chile con carne that'll

[9]

make a man forget he ever et before, and tortillas as thin as the blade of your Green River."

"Is that all she can do?" sang out Sam Lash.

"Nossir! That ain't all she can do and it ain't
all she's gonna do, neither. Get along, you goddam mule! Cain't you see that gal awaitin'?"

Down the west slope where the snow melts
first everything was alive and the lower they went
the more life showed. White-stemmed aspen was
budding into leaf, brush along the canyon was
greening and the creek roared over its banks with
yellow water running straight from melting snow.
Great blue fool-hens boomed up beside the trail
and perched tame in tall dark spruce trees silver-
tipped with the new year's growth. Blue jays
squabbled and screamed among the trees in fluttering couples and little red squirrels raced and
chattered. Now and then a blacktail buck with
sprouting knobbly antlers bounced out of the
brush and up the mountain in long stiff-legged
hops. Once they came on a black bear digging wild
onions and he woofed and scampered making
their pack mules snort and swerve.

They stopped for nothing. At noon they
chewed jerked meat they had in their pockets and
drank muddy water lying flat by the creek. At
sunset they were down at the foot of the mountains where the low bunchy piñon grew sparse like

apple trees in an orchard. Grass was thick and six inches high and flowers were blooming red yellow and blue, bright as Indian paint. With a hook and line he had in his hat and slugs he found under a log Sam Lash fished in the eddies along the edge of the swollen creek and pulled out big trout. They had dark coppergreen backs with black spots, salmon-pink sides and bone white bellies. They fell flopping in the grass and danced themselves to death. Over the fire they curled and popped showing white meat fine as clotted cream.

This was safe country, so they turned the mules loose on good forage and slept without a guard by a big red fire.

They were up and riding by dawn along the edge of the hills where the timber peters out and the blue sage begins and spreads west to the gorge of the Rio Grande. Prairie dogs were out of the ground, upright and chirping beside their mounds, jerking nervous tails. Badgers threw up fresh dirt from their underground hunting and stuck out grizzled noses stained with clay and blood. Jack-rabbits sat tame and lazy beside the trail, the sunrise shining pink through their tall ears. Away off to the west antelope galloped and wheeled and their white rump patches flashed in the sun.

Late in the afternoon they topped a rise and

saw Taos valley green with new crops and the brown huddle of the town among cottonwood trees.

Taos was a place where Indians and Mexicans had lived since God knows when. It was the first place north of Santa Fe where you could throw a spree and the first place south of Bent's Fort on the Arkansas where you could sell beaver.

Taos was a place where corn grew and women lived.

Soon or late every man in the mountains came to Taos. They came to it from as far north as the Red and as far south as the Gila. They came to it like buffalo to a salt lick across thousands of dangerous miles. Taos whiskey and Taos women were known and talked about on every beaver stream in the Rockies. More than any other place Taos was the heart of the mountains.

When they saw Taos they rose in their stirrups and let a yell.

First they came to the Indian pueblo three miles from the town. It rose in two five-storied blocks of brown adobe on either side of a bright stream shining through budded willow brush. The mountains lifted east of it and westward spread farm lands where brown men were scratching the earth with wooden plows, digging sakeys and singing to their gods while they worked. The whole town was out in the sun. Red skirted bare-footed women were on the roofs and in front of the houses, bending over baskets, kettles and hides. Young girls were plastering walls, silver bracelets and rings flashing through mud they laid on with long smooth strokes. They stopped and smiled over shoulders at the riding men and some of the bolder waved. Lean dogs and dirty pa-pooses scattered away from the road.

They waved and shouted and clattered on.

Four men that had stopped at the pueblo to trade swung into their saddles and galloped to join them. They were mountain men, too—Marcelline the Mexican and Chabonard from Canada and Pegleg Smith and Black Harris. They shouted greetings without a stop and rode on in a cavalcade through the Indian lands.

Wild plum bushes piled white blossom along the sakeys, sun-freed waters ran noisily to sprouting crops and the air was full of a spring smell.

When they struck the gate of the town someone started the Indian chant they always chanted when they rode in bunches feeling good.

"Hai, hai, hai!" he chanted. "Hai yai, hai yai, hai yai!"

They all took it up and chanted it to the rumble of their riding.

"Hai, hai, hai! Hai yai, hai yai, hai yai!"

[13]

Around the plaza brown men slouched sulky and resentful in doorways, with serapes pulled up and sombreros pulled down, with corn husk cigarettes hanging from secretive mouths. More came out from bars and stores and stood and looked. Some got up from squatting comfort against shady walls and some left games of coon-can, but none gave a greeting.

A cockfight at the corner, that was right in the way, blew up into running cursing men and fluttering squawking birds.

The mountain men rode straight through it and saved some rooster's life.

Out of the way, you greasers! You can't shine now!

Here come mountain men hell-bent for a spree!

Barelegged women, passing with water jars and baskets on their heads, stopped and looked shyly delighted and other women ran to doors and peered and ogled and from tiny windows and barely opened *portales* of great houses even *rico* women peeped with eager eyes. How Mexican women loved hard-riding, Indian-killing gringos, full of lust and money!

Ho, you *muchachas,* get ready for big doins!

Wash off the red stain of *alegria* that saves your faces from the sun.

[14]

Put on your bright red skirts and white *camisas*.

Hang silver and gold on your necks and arms.
Limber your legs for dancing and wear roses
in your hair.

Here come mountain men hell-bent for a spree!

CHAPTER TWO

I

AM LASH grew up in a log house in western Kentucky, where his father was among the first to build and plow.

Inside were puncheon floor, straw tick and copper kettle, hoe cake and hominy and wild game for meat.

Outside the corn sprang tall from black loam where the forest had fallen and all around the snake fence the forest still stood.

He heard bob-white in the morning and whippoor-will at dusk and sometimes in the night he heard a panther scream.

He remembered when men carried rifles to the corn field and a brother crawling home bloody with arrows in his back and a wet scalp thrown down with curses. He knew always that brown skin was to shoot at and Indian hair to lift.

He remembered arms of his mother holding him a little while and her voice telling him about a white house in Virginia and niggers and tobacco

[16]

fields—telling him sadly he was gentlefolks, half
way at least. But she could not hold him long for
he was the middle child of twelve. She had more
babies and the ague and all her own work to do.
Worn and weary she pushed him away and he ran
wild, uncombed and dirty. But he remembered
arms holding him and a great white house and he
knew he was gentlefolks half way at least.

2

Through the tall corn went little tow-headed
Sam armed with a rifle longer than himself stolen
from the rack while the men were away. He went
to the woods that had called him ever since he
could walk. Black oak, sweet gum, hickory and
tulip tree grew on the high ground and down
along the bottoms sycamore, elm and water maple
laced long branches over the creek. Jumping deer
flaunted white tails and vanished. Wild turkeys
yelped and ran. Gray squirrels and fox squirrels,
raiding the corn, flashed along fence rails and up
trees. Partridges thundered up under his feet and
he saw the myriads of the wild pigeons break limbs
off trees with their fluttering burden.

Little Sam Lash hunted like a hound pup for
it was in his blood to hunt and the earth swarmed
with game for his taking.

A lean blond buck in hickory and homespun he went to husking parties, log-rollings, hay rides. He fought rough and tumble for the fun of it, drank forty rod and apple-jack and swung girls in the Virginia reel while fiddles played Turkey in the Straw. He found girls liked him and he liked them. He rolled one in a haystack and another in a corn field and it was only luck he wasn't married or shot. The girls called him wild and hard to catch and liked him the better for that.

3

Everything was moving West right past the door. Conestoga wagons went through almost every day bound for the river and the Indian country beyond. One after another his big brothers went West. Sam's mother, hoping to hold him, put him in a blacksmith shop. He hammered tires and shoes and mended swingle-trees and tongues and heard waiting men tell about beaver and buffalo, Arapaho, Cheyenne and Comanche, Santa Fe and the Mexican trade—about mountains unmapped and enormous.

Sam only waited until he had a hundred dollars. Then he headed West as a goose heads north in spring. He dreamed of wild country and of himself in buckskin on a horse, of fine fights and easy money and towns to blow it in, but chiefly he followed the crowd and the hunch that was in him.

St. Louis was booming when he hit it. Long rows of paddle wheel ships nosed up to the docks and singing shouting niggers swung the loads. For the first time in his life Sam Lash walked among crowds agape and delighted. Corncrackers in homespun and high boots geehawed their mule teams in cluttered muddy streets, cracked eight foot whips and squirted tobacco juice from bulging jaws. Traders full of corn liquor and easy money swelled around in boiled shirts, long-tailed coats of bright color and beaver hats big as buckets, with rings on their fingers and heavy gold chains across their gaudy vests. They rolled big cigars in their mouths and treated each other noisily in reeking bars. Women in bright ballooning silks rolled by in phaëtons and coaches. Such women Sam had never seen before. Dark soft women out of *vide poche* with velvet skins and round arms and necks and helpless hands, looking and smelling like great flowers, they seemed hardly of the same sex as the shrill thin busy women he had mostly known.

Far more than women, men in buckskin filled his eye—men out of the mountains! They were men of many breeds—dark French Canadians blond lanky Missourians of his own kind, a few

Swedes and Englishmen and a few Mexicans—
but all were alike in buckskin and sunburn, in
long hair and smooth face, in lean hard-bitten
strength and swaggering independence. They
came from a place where fat men, fools and cow-
ards cannot live.

Sam Lash, hating his baggy homespun and his
coonskin cap, trailed them to Hawkins gun shop
and put most of his money into a rifle twice as
heavy as he had ever held, guaranteed to shoot
plum center and throw a buffalo in his tracks. He
trailed them to the Rocky Mountain House, where
all of them hung out and he sat in the bar listening to their lies. More and more came as it got
later and liquor ran free.

Men threw silver dollars in clattering handfuls
on the bar and stood treat to all comers. Sam Lash
was a comer every time till he felt like a mountain
man himself. He wanted to tell 'em all that he
could bark a squirrel as far as he could see one,
that he could lick any man his weight and that
he'd never been scared in his life.

Fiddles played and yellow girls from *vide poche*
were on the floor. Men grabbed them and danced,
each his own way, whooping with delight.

A corner wouldn't hold Sam Lash any longer.
He got out in the middle and did a break-down
while the crowd patted and stamped and whooped

him on. Then he grabbed for a girl that had taken his eye. He thought he owned the house.

A fist cracked on his jaw. He fell ten feet away but came up fighting, vaguely aware of a crowd falling back, of shouts and of a bloody face before him that he longed to smash. Then something hit him from behind and the world exploded into smithereens of colored light and subsided into oblivion.

He waked up the next morning with a head he could hardly move and a woman he couldn't remember beside him.

4

Forty new Conestogas, painted blue and red, with new white covers shining in the sun, sat in a circle waiting for the start while forty breakfast camp fires sent up blue smoke.

Widehorned oxen were rounded up on the prairie, poured into the circle of wagons, milling in their dust. Hickory-shirted teamsters sorted and yoked them yelling wo-has and curses. Owners climbed into light Springfield carriages and trotted on ahead. Hunters swung into saddles. Shouts went round the circle, whips cracked, and the train stretched and crawled.

Sam Lash trudged beside a rut and prodded a laboring steer.

They crossed a rolling country where the cut banks of the creeks showed deep black soil, where grass brushed a horse's belly and sunflower and golden-rod grew rank and high. Tall timber hid running water and grew in topes on hilltops. Deer bounded in the bottoms and prairie chicken rumbled up and skimmed the grass. It was a country where a man might have plowed and built anywhere and lived fat the rest of his life, but instead men cut the sod with hooves and wheels, making a road to the West.

There were a few cabins at first but the farther they went the wilder it was. Sam Lash saw deer and elk in far off bottoms standing like cattle knee deep in shaded water, thrashing at flies. Antelope began to show, skimming over the high spots, vanishing into the shimmer of sunlight on widening horizons. Wolves and coyotes trailed the wagons, trotting warily far off, waiting for night to come nearer and pick up leavings.

Daily the country lifted and flattened, faded from green to pale gray and yellow, stretched desolate and enormous so far it hurt the eye to look. Trees were gone and rivers were bone white sand. Game was scarce and water was far between.

It seemed to Sam Lash they would never get anywhere—as though they moved against a space too great to conquer.

Water and chuck was short and so was talk. Everyone was tired and empty. Sun, dust and distance beat heavily upon their spirits. War parties of Osages, with their faces painted black and their shaved scalps vermillion, sat their horses and watched but were afraid. Some rode into camp to beg and got nothing but curses. Sam Lash took long tired turns at guarding the cavvayard, riding lonely circles round the sleeping stock with the yip and bicker of coyotes in his ears and visions of sneaking Indians pricking him awake.

Storms struck them, piling up black with thunder and lightning, exploding into a rush of great hailstones that killed a picketed horse and drove men under wagons. An arroyo that had been bone dry rushed in a red wide flood across their way and wagons bogged in the mud of its wake.

One morning they saw far away prairie spotted to the horizon with black things thick as huckleberries on a bush. The black things moved and massed and a shout went up from one end of the train to the other. Hurrah for the meat!

With wide eyes and pounding blood, Sam Lash saw buffalo—black solid acres of wild beef moving in a rumble that shook the earth. He saw hunters put out on restless horses, heard the boom of heavy rifles, and the train came up with men bloody to the elbows, piling red meat on steaming

[23]

hides, sorting chocolate-colored livers out of purple piles of guts, cutting tongues out of huge
shaggy heads.

That night they gathered around fires and
gorged and joked, greasy blades flashing over
limitless humprib, fleece and tongue. Wild meat
put new life into them all so that they sang
and shouted and fiddles were brought out and
stories told. All were happy but especially the
buckskinned men from the mountains. "Ho boy,"
they shouted to each other, "it's good to be among
the meat again. Hurrah for the mountain doins!"

Lying that night with a full belly by a dying
fire, sucking on a pipe, Sam Lash felt content. He
was glad to be half way to nowhere. Home for
him was to lie beside a road.

5

Alien jobless and ragged he wandered the
streets of the mudtown they called Taos. Flat
square houses made of yellow dirt huddled all inside one high protecting wall, bunched around a
treeless public square full of dust, dogs and beggars, saddle horses dozing on three legs, loafers
propped against shady walls staring at brown
bare-legged women who padded by with water
jars on their heads.

It smelled of dust, horses, sweat and wine. At evening it tinkled with hidden music and always it pattered softly in a strange tongue.

It was a lazy place where everyone seemed waiting for something, not caring when it came, a dirty place, an earth town earth-soiled, giving up to the warmth of the sun its own peculiar defiant stench of life lived in sensuous untroubled squalor.

To the stranger it was a place hostile with the deadly hostility of indifference. It hid its life away behind walls three feet thick in cool dark cavelike rooms and invisible courts. It showed him little mica-set iron-barred windows and great double doors swung on heavy hinges. Through them, briefly opened, he glimpsed the rich kernel of the town's life in the great sprawling houses where owners of sheep and slaves lived fat lazy lives. He glimpsed pretty women in flowered patios and Indian slaves bearing silver dishes. Hungrily he smelled meat, chocolate and wine. He saw tall-hatted men ride out on shining horses. Often their saddles were silver mounted and they wore silver spurs. They rode with proud-lifted heads and did not look at him.

Only the priest looked at him.

The priest had a great house, too, with an orchard behind it. He was a tall young man with a saddle-yellow hawk-nosed face and long legs that fought his robe. He met Sam Lash on a corner, stopped him and spoke to him in good English, asking him where he came from and what he did there. Sam Lash said he came from the Missouri and was looking for work. The priest looked at him hard as a man looks at a strange new thing he knows he must deal with. He gave him work picking apples in the shady orchard and afterward a girl called him into a long kitchen where a red savory mess stewed in an iron kettle. She brought him an earthen bowl of it and a stack of thin hot wheaten cakes that she made on a stone griddle. Sam Lash was weak with hunger but he didn't know how to begin. There was no spoon nor fork. The girl laughed at him and rolled a cake into a cup and dipped it full of stew and put it in his hands. He crammed it greedily into his mouth and then his eyes went blind with sudden tears and his tongue seemed on fire. It was his first taste of red chile which stings a strange palate like a bee.

While the girl laughed at him he wavered whether to swallow or spew but finally he swallowed and she applauded.

"Bueno, gringo, bueno," she shouted.

Sam Lash paid her no attention. Food comes before women. He went back at his scarlet mutton and with a burning but indomitable mouth he devoured it to the last morsel. Then he wiped his lips and eyes and leaned back and filled and lit a pipe and looked at the girl who sat on a bench across the room. Squat, wide-hipped and full-bosomed, she grinned at him with all her teeth, swung a bare foot and lifted a pretty hand to heavy plaited hair like a horse's mane. Sam Lash rose lazily and walked about the room pointing at dish, door, window. She understood. She gave him the Spanish word for each and he named it over three times and knew then it was his. When he had learned everything else in the room he sat down beside the girl and touched her hand and she said "mano," giggling. He stroked her arm and the unexpected Indian softness of her flesh stirred his blood, but he did not forget to learn that arm is *brazo*. Then he hitched closer and laid a gentle hand on her neck. She shivered and laughed and wriggled reluctantly away from his following eager hand. . . .

The priest thundered at them suddenly from the doorway, standing there tall and black, roaring his rage after the scampering wench. Sam Lash stood up to face him but when the girl was gone the padre put off his rage like a shirt. He wiped his brow and grinned at his guest. Then he laid a silver dollar on the table jerked his thumb at the door and was off after the errant one.

That night Sam crouched in a doorway and watched them dance—*caballeros* in flaring pants, buckskinned hunters with bright new shirts on, women of the street and women out of the great houses in gaudy *camisas* and *rebosos*. The priest was there and none swung the girls any better than he.

Candles lit blue smoke from corn husk *cigarillos* and a little drunken fiddler rocked and sawed and made the whole room hop.

One girl was taller than any of the others and she wore a scarlet shawl and had black hair piled high and her white neck lifted sweetly.

In the doorway sprawled dirty boys and a few beggars—and Sam Lash, dirty and ragged as any.

Beggars sprawled idle, waiting a dole, but Sam Lash crouched tense, full of hunger, hope and envy.

Sprout of a conquering race he squatted ragged among beggars and greedily took with his eyes all that he saw.

Women, gold and silver, slaves and wine were his. A great house firm as the earth, stored with fat living, comforted his driven homeless spirit. The tall whitefleshed girl stood naked in his imagination and her body bent to his will.

6

The only job that he could get was going back
the way he came. Once more he trudged beside
oxen in choking dust and shouted woha, and saw
the mountains sink into the earth behind him.
But half way across he got a job with a wagon
train headed for Taos, and back to mudtown
he went, knowing he must but hardly knowing
why.

More than a year he spent in journeys, a vaga-
bond between jobs, learning language and country. Then in the second spring when mountain
men were putting out for the fur country, a man
named Wyeth who had worked with Jim Bridger in the North, organized a party in Taos to
trap the southern streams. One more man he
needed and one more man was hard to get for
beaver was six dollars a pound and almost every
trapper was in the field either on his own or working for one of the big companies.

The one more man he finally found was a
lanky towheaded bullwhacker, twenty-one years
old and green as the new grass. His name was
Sam Lash and his assets were one Hawkins rifle
and the ragged homespun he wore. Wyeth took
him because he had a good gun, could talk Mex
and was red and stuttering with eagerness.

7

Twenty men and fifty horses strung out on the westward trail. Missouri Yankees, Canadian half breeds, one Swede, an Englishman and two Delaware Indians made the crew. Sam Lash rode at the rear eating the dust of travel. His job was to wrangle the stock and keep the pack mules moving.

They headed west and north to fool the greasers for they were out to trap Mexican territory without a license. In the tilted pine-clad mesas of the San Juan country they turned south past Inscription Rock and the ice caves through a barren land where rivers of lava lamed their horses and great red and purple buttes rose out of the desert. They saw the mud hogans and the pied sheep herds of the Navajo and with cocked rifles they traded beads and knives to tall warriors for red and black blankets so tight-woven they would hold water. They struck the Rio Grande again below Socorro where the river, thick with mud, cut through wide cottonwood bottoms. Buds were just beginning to swell, spring fur was still prime, and beaver sign was everywhere. Now Sam Lash learned to read sign. He learned to anchor a trap and bait it with the medicine he carried in a horn bottle, to set a float stick and flesh and stretch a pelt. His days were all work and study. He had everything to learn. He had to learn his business of taking fur. He had to learn strange country and the sign language that was the only common language of the mountains. And everything he learned he had to carry in his head.

They summered in the White Mountains and for three months he had life easy in a high cool country where clear streams full of trout poured down from the peaks, grass was thick in the canyons and deer hid in the heavy spruce. They hunted just enough to eat, made moccasins and shirts and sprawled in groups telling yarns and gambling for everything they had. Strong friend ships grew in idleness and bickering enmities exploded into bloody fights when noses and ears were bitten and eyes gouged while an eager circle watched till one man cried for mercy.

Here Sam Lash proved himself, made himself over in the mountain pattern. He fought and held his own and walked respected. He hunted and brought in more than his share of meat. He became known to all for one who could hold a track across dry ground like an Indian and plant a ball where he wanted it. He made himself buckskin shirt and pants, traded for moccasins and a beaded pipe case to hang around his neck and a flat black hat. He scraped his face and let his yellow hair hang long and tangled to his shoulders. He walked swaggering in the pride of young power. He was a mountain man—wagh!

When quaking asp turned yellow they trapped down the Salido, starting in tiny streams up near timberline, following the prime fur to the lower levels. When snow covered the mountains behind them they were down where the Gila runs through sand and greasewood in a desolate country spotted with ruins of great stone houses built by Indians of long ago.

Riding careless in the strength of twenty rifles they ran into a war party of Apaches driving a hundred horses stolen from the Mexican settlements of the Rio Grande. Yelling they charged. Apaches whooped back at them and showered arrows from under their horses' necks while the stolen herd stampeded at the crash of rifle fire. Red men with bows and arrows scattered and ran before white men with rifles.

Sam Lash came late to camp that night with a wet scalp at his belt and plunder of beaded moccasins and turquoise and an Apache arrow sticking in his leg. He sat proud at the fire with blood of a man on his hands while they butchered the arrow out of his flesh and bandaged him with beaver fur and buckskin. After that a Mexican boy took over the cavvayard. Sam Lash was a warrior.

They rounded up the horses and each man took what he could use. Young fat horses they killed and ate and the rest they turned loose again.

When the fur season was over Wyeth held a pow-wow and told them he was all set to go to California, trap the coast streams and hit the missions. Only two parties had ever done it before. No one knew how far it was or how to get there. Thirsty desert was on the way. Those that wanted to go could stand up and those that were minded to head back for Taos with the beaver packs could sit still. Sam Lash was one that stood.

8

Ten men rode north and west from the Gila without a trail. The country was flat sunbitten mesa thinly timbered with piñon and cedar, cut deep in red gashes of arroyo where water ought to have been but wasn't. They stopped to hunt and ten men in a hard day got only three deer. They jerked the meat and went on.

Now Sam Lash learned what it was to go two days and two nights without water, to feel his tongue swell and fill his mouth like a dry rag, to see the trees dance jigs on the hilltops, to drink the blood that runs thick and purple from the throat of a slaughtered horse and gag and drink again. Water when they found it was often in stinking pools patrolled by buzzards with drowned pack rats and prairie dogs floating in a green scum . . . They drank it and filled the long gut of a horse with it, Apache fashion, and went on.

Sam Lash learned now that meat is meat. He learned to chew moccasin leather for supper and kill a rattle-snake and eat him roasted over the coals for breakfast. He tasted prairie dog and ground squirrel and learned that the meat of a young coyote is white and tender and makes a man think of pork and hominy and hoe cake and women—makes a man curse the day he left home. . . . They ate what they could kill and went on.

After ten days they came to the great canyon they had heard of—a canyon a mile deep and ten miles wide cut through red and yellow rock—a canyon that made a man feel like a flea. From a point they could see a red wide river in the bottom and green patches that looked like growing crops. It took them days to find a trail down. Most of the way they slid and pack horses fell and rolled and broke their necks but finally they lay flat beside the river drinking gallons of red water. Next day they came to a Mojave village and tall dark warriors, dressed in colored cottons of their own weaving, came gravely suspicious to meet them. They traded for black beans, corn and squash seeds, killed fat colts for meat, gorged and rested. Then they crossed the river on log rafts, swimming their horses, and went on.

Up the Mojave River they had good water and some game but little Digger Indians that lived in woven greasewood huts hung to their trail, hiding in the rocks by day, raiding the cavvayard at night.

Dirty, black-handed from grubbing in the earth, hardly ever five feet high, they never rode horses but stole them only to kill. They were worse than Indians that would ride and fight. They came at night and shot poisoned arrows and when they were chased they ran chattering like monkeys up rocky hillsides where a horse could not follow.

Finally they surprised a Digger village, drove scampering dwarfs out of dusty brush hovels, ducked their poisoned darts, shot down three men and roped two little screaming squaws. Other plunder there was none but bags of dried ants and shrivelled roots they couldn't eat and meat of their own horses blackening in the sun on a jerking frame.

One of the squaws ran away in the night. Big Bill Harp claimed the other, said he was half-froze for woman. . . . But when he laid a hand on her she bit him so he bled. He would have killed her in a spasm of rage—they told of him that he killed and ate a Yamparica squaw in the starving country west of the great salt lake—but Jack Lucien, a French Canadian half breed, laid him flat with a chunk of wood and took the squaw away from him. Little by little he tamed her with food as one tames a half-wild dog, till she crawled to his blankets at night, dressed skins for him, chewing buckskin soft, dug strange roots for him and baked them in the ashes. He refused an offer of a good horse and fifty dollars for her.

At the head of the Mojave they crossed low mountains and dropped into a wide grassy valley that seemed almost too pretty to be real after what they had been through. Oak trees spread wide shade over high grass and water ran clear. They saw great herds of half-wild cattle and horses that belonged to the missions with half-wild Indians herding them, killing what they wanted to eat. Then they came to San Gabriel with its adobe walls and wooden cross standing high over orchards of olives, figs, and cherries. A priest of enormous belly, barefooted, in a goatskin tunic, gave them an uneasy welcome of fear and squat Indian women fed them chile con carne, tortillas, fruit and even coffee.

On to the pueblo of Los Angeles they went, where a thousand people lived in low flat adobe houses roofed with asphalt that welled up from the ground. They sold beaver secretly against the Mexican law, bribing the *alcalde,* got howling drunk on red wine, broke up fandangos with their barbarous dancing, knocking greasers off the floor, having their own way with women. . . . No one wanted trouble with ten mountain men.

North they rode to the San Joaquin, taking all the horses they wanted from the mission herds, trapping streams that had never been touched by steel, loading their animals with bales of peltry.

They rode conquering, gathering wealth, through a country soft and fat where nothing stood against their hard-bitten hazard-loving strength. And yet none of them wanted to stay. After nights and days of feasting, red wine and women they craved saddle leather and a change of scene. In September they headed East again, up the beaver streams.

9

When Sam Lash hit Bent's Fort on the Arkansas that winter he was a mountain man complete. He owned four horses and two hundred dollars. Before he blew his money he bought traps and a

[37]

rucksack, Green River knives, powder and lead and Virginia leaf tobacco. With a good store of these he was his own man for months and his own man he planned to remain. He was going it alone as a free trapper.

He did not stay at the fort a week. He could stay nowhere. He could stand anything but comfort. He could do anything but rest. He lived a life of starvation and liked it. When he hit a town, a trading post or a rendez-vous he was a creature of crying needs. He was hungry for the taste of bread and sugar. He was hungry for the feel and voice of women. He craved the madness and oblivion of liquor. Riding into a town he felt as though he could crunch its gathered human sweetness between his teeth. And after a few days he would wake up poor and sick, hating the smell of huddled sheltered men, longing for moun-tains.

Mountains had laid their spell on him as they did on all of his ilk. Mountains were his work and his passion. Tiny and unafraid he crawled over the broad backs of unconquerable mountains, lay down and slept in their sheltering folds. For months at a stretch he ate nothing but meat that he killed and spoke to none but his horses.

He had suffered all the cruelties of mountains.

They had starved him and frozen him. They had buried him in snows and drenched him with storms. He knew the gloomy half-madness that falls on long solitudes when a man hates himself and the echo of his own voice, and images of desire dog him all day and lie down with him at night and the half-human scream of a mountain lion makes him twitch.

He knew the sweetness of camp on good grass and water when full-bellied horses stand just outside the fire-red circle and the smell of roasting meat mingles with smoke in the nose.

He knew the passionate fellowship of men riding and hunting together, fighting together in bloody brutal play, sitting round fires swapping yarns of wild beasts and women and other strange creatures that are found in a world of mountains and men.

He knew all the great game of the Rockies—buffalo and antelope that winter in the lower valleys, elk that run over the high ridges in black-necked herds, deer and bear, black and grizzly, and the wild sheep that range to the tops of the highest peaks. He had killed and eaten them all. He was flesh of their flesh—a man nourished on wildness.

Sam Lash had found his trade and he knew his destiny.

He knew a mountain man goes on until he gets rubbed out.

10

He went North in the spring because he had been South before. Sometimes alone, sometimes with two or three he trapped the Blackfoot country at the headwaters of the Yellowstone and the Missouri, saw the strange places Jim Bridger had found, and learned of his own eyes that Jim Bridger hadn't lied when he told of boiling springs that would cook meat and a spouting river that threw water seventy feet in the air.

He took many a pack of beaver in those few years when beaver were thick in the streams and worth almost their weight in silver on the market because every gentleman had to have a beaver hat.

To crown gentlemen with beaver hats mountain men worked out every canyon from the Gila to the Columbia, mapped the mountains in their minds, killed Indians and learned their languages and their ways. In the Southwest they went everywhere the Spaniards had never dared to go and in the Northwest they found country that none had ever seen.

For their share of the earth they took mountains that were considered forever dead to civilization, an impassable barrier between seas. And they took it because they liked it. All the money they made out of beaver they spent and most of them left their bones in the mountains.

Sam Lash saw many times the great rendezvous when mountain men, Indians and traders met for a day of business and a week of carnival. He was at Brown's Hole and on the Laramie and at Green River. He was at the Salt Lake rendezvous when a hundred mountain men and two thousand Snake Indians beat the Blackfeet in a two day fight and General Ashley came out from St. Louis with fifty mules packed for trade, about half of them with liquor.

That was the biggest doings he ever saw. The white Snake lodges dotted a circle a mile wide and mountain men and traders were camped all around them. Night and day the Indian village was filled with the yelp and rumble of naked painted Snakes dancing the scalp dance around the bloody hair of slaughtered Blackfeet hung from poles. Everybody, white and red, was in liquor. The Traders were pouring it out free to make their goods move faster. Fights were so many a man could hardly decide which one to watch. Most of them were bloody rough-and-tumbles between men too drunk to shoot, but there were duels with rifles at fifty paces and one where both men went under.

Up and down a course before the lodges incessant horse races lifted a yellow fog of dust. Indians rode naked, arms and legs going, whipping and yelling from start to finish. White men in buckskin rode low and silent in their saddles beating better Indian horses by craft and skill, taking the stakes of peltry, robe and gun piled up at the end of the track.

Games of sevenup and monte were going big. Some men were gathering more gear than they could pack and some lost horse and beaver and some went away without their shirts.

Young Snake squaws were out in all their *fofarraw* with white men bidding against red for them. Squat bandy-legged girls with wide grinning faces, deep bosoms and soft brown skins, they rode up and down dressed in yellow antelope hide tanned soft as velvet, trimmed with blue beads, porcupines quills and polished elk teeth. Their ponies tinkled with many little brass bells hung in manes and tails.

It was a squaw that saved Sam Lash from losing all he had in games and liquor. He could never keep his eyes off women and one Snake girl became the whole show to him. He trailed her to her father's lodge and paraded before the old man's eyes such wealth of ponies and robes, beads and knives that he took the girl away with him.

She was afraid at first. She had a crazy Indian
notion that a man with yellow hair and a white
skin was a god and bad medicine for a woman
and she shrank away from his hand. But when she
found that he was a man and good medicine she
stuck to him like a dog and worked for him as he
had never been worked for in all his life.

He set up housekeeping in the mountain
fashion with a Snake lodge he bought and a
travois. His Mountain Flower put up the lodge
single-handed and set the top vents so that her
cooking fire never filled it with smoke. When they
moved she took it down again and packed it on the
travois and drove the pony with shrill shouts of
Ya krashne. She tanned buffalo robes for him as
only an Indian can, scraping them thin with an elk-
horn scraper and working them soft as wool. She
dried *kinnik-kinnik* and mixed it with his tobacco
to make the favorite mountain smoke. She bought
woolly dogs and raised puppies to make him stews,
feeding them fat till they were just the right age
and then strangling them with a bow string as
coolly as a farmer's wife wrings a chicken's neck.

She was a great comfort in winter quarters with
her skill at keeping a lodge warm and her stores
of jerked meat and buffalo paunches stuffed with
fat and marrow. She took care of the horses, cutting cottonwood browse for them when snows

buried the grass, hopping about like a magpie in the tree tops. She went on awful rampages sometimes and shouted Snake curses at him so fast he couldn't trail her, but he soon found that at such times all she wanted was a lodge-poling and after he had hit her a few wallops she would be docile and happy again.

When he struck for the high mountains in the spring he thought he would have to find some place to leave her so he could move faster, but he might as well have tried to leave his left foot. She could go anywhere he could. When they pushed into country where a *travois* couldn't drag she packed the lodge on a pony and when they had to go lighter still she cached it and they lived in wickiups she built with brush and a couple of robes.

She fitted so easily into his life he hardly knew she was there. She was less a woman than part of the outfit like the pack mules and his rifle. . . .

On the head of Green River a herd of mountain buffalo stampeded his mules and he had to trail them all day and sleep out that night. When he got back to camp with them the second afternoon, Mountain Flower and wickiup were gone— gone were horses, beaver traps and robes and the broad trail of a Blackfoot war party showed what had happened. Mountain Flower had gone the way of most good squaws.

He was alone with a handful of powder and eight rifle balls two hundred miles from the nearest fort.

Two weeks later he struck Bent's poor and ragged with only one mule to his name because he had eaten the other. There he got powder, ball and traps on credit and pitched in with Thatcher and Gullion to make his fortune again. They agreed before they started they would sell their fur in Taos.

Sam Lash had hankered for Taos ever since he had left it. He wanted to hit it again and he wanted to hit it flush. He wanted to call on the padre when he didn't need a meal or a job picking apples and he wanted to walk into a *baile* and show the greasers they couldn't shine when a mountain man was among them. . . .

CHAPTER THREE

I

OLA SALAZAR woke about sunrise and lay listening to the sounds of her father's house as it began to stir. She heard low lazy voices of Indian women talking and laughing, the whispering of moccasined feet along the ground as they crossed the *placita* bearing jars of water on their heads from the well, the splash and rattle of beginning activity in the kitchen. Behind the house a stallion neighed, men laughed and swore, creaking cart wheels started for the farms.

All these familiar sounds came sweetly to her ears for they were the voice of a life that moved in well-known ways bearing her easily along. They soothed her and a little they bored her.

Presently she forgot them and began thinking about her chocolate—thick brown chocolate, beady with fat beaten to froth in a copper bowl by old Consuelo who was an artist of chocolate and did nothing but make it. She was also think-

[46]

ing of *sopapillas* and how they collapse under the teeth into tender crumbling sweetness. Lola Salazar enjoyed eating as only the idle can, looking lovingly forward to each of the long procession of meals that marched out of her father's kitchen in silver dishes borne on brown arms of women he owned. In a few minutes her own maid, Abrana, would bring her *sopapillas* and chocolate and that would have to last her until nine o'clock when the family would meet for a breakfast of mutton, hot bread filled with sugar and spice and coffee served with hot milk. Then she would have her work to do of doling out supplies in the kitchen and setting the women their tasks, but about eleven she would take a bowl of broth or a cup of chocolate to keep up her strength until the middle of the day when dinner was served. Two kinds of meat they would have then —a roast of mutton or beef and a stew of jerked buffalo meat with red chile or perhaps a boiled chicken, and there would be white heaps of steamed rice, cabbages, spinach and other garden vegetables and a custard pudding for dessert with raisins and *pinones* scattered through its yellow richness to surprise the teeth. They would all eat slowly and elegantly without knives, picking up meat in their fingers and tossing bits of bone and gristle daintily over their shoulders to be caught by well-trained dogs. They would sit a long time talking idly about trifles and sipping red wine from silver cups. After that she would retire to her siesta for the hot hours of the summer afternoon when even slaves did not work and dogs and horses dozed in the shade and birds were quiet in the trees and the breeze dropped. About four in the afternoon when the men rode in from the *ranchos,* they would all meet in the *sala* for chocolate and sweet cakes and would talk again until supper time. Her cousin and suitor, Ambrosio Guiterrez, would be there and he would perhaps bring his guitar and sing her a new *verso* he had made. Only he never really made *versos,* but took of the thousands that had already been made and changed them a little and sang them prettily. All of them were about his soul and his heart and about her hair and her eyes and her arms. Having started with her hair and worked as far down as her arms he had to work up again. She was getting a little tired of Ambrosio's *versos.*

> They say black is the color of sorrow
> And I say it cannot be true,
> For black is the color of your eyes
> And all of my joy is in you.

It was pretty good but it was old and she had heard better. Tircio Romero, her first love, had made *versos* that were wholly his own and had even written *inditas* and longer songs. He was killed by Apaches on his way to Sonora to buy her a maid and she was always sad when she thought of him although it was two years ago and already she found it hard to summon his face. His blond hair she remembered because so few people she knew had blond hair and she remembered the lines he had sung for her before he started on the last trip of his life.

> I wander far and I wander long
> And my home is where I find me,
> But I would never wander more
> If your white arms would bind me.

And Tircio was a wanderer, a restless fellow like a gringo, who could not sit still for more than a couple of hours and was full of great plans for a new settlement farther north. Many had predicted that he would be killed.

She had met him at her first dance and had fallen in love with his blond hair and he had hung around the house most of the time after that until he went away on his last trip.

She had never seen him alone. She had never been alone with any man and never would be until she was married.

Lola was guarded from men and from the

world by a tradition centuries old that had come
unchanged across the ocean. She was part of an
ancient stream of woman-feeling that sensuous
men had long guarded behind thick walls and
barred windows, keeping it pure and dangerous
for their delight.

When Tircio came to the house in the evenings
they sang songs and played games—the whole
family and their visitors together. One game they
played was called Molina. Each one took for
himself the name of a part of a mill and one who
stood up told a story about a mill and at a certain
point in the story the mill was broken all to pieces.
Then everyone had to jump up and scramble for
a new seat and whoever got left was the next
storyteller. In the scramble hands touched and
swift meaning looks were traded.

Once when they played Molina she had run
plump into the arms of Tircio with a shock that
drove blood into her ears and made her knees
wobble.

Now the blond hair of Tircio hung from an
Apache belt and Ambrosio had taken his place in
the *sala* and sat waiting to marry her. He had
gone for her father on a trading trip to Sonora as
was the custom and had brought her back an
Indian maid. The marriage had been arranged
by their parents. It would take place soon and

would have taken place already if she had not begged them to postpone it.

Ever since the death of Tircio she had sometimes flown into rages at nothing, slapped her maid and wept. Ever since then the sleepy peacefulness of life had bored her. She was tired of droning voices of women at work, priests chanting litanies, lovers singing *versos* and twanging guitars, turtle doves mourning in cottonwood trees. She had terrible dreams of flying through windows like a witch and falling through limitless spaces. She dreamed of Tircio crowned with blood and smiling at her with a dead smile and of Apaches chasing her with scalping knives. Time and again she dreamed of violence and blood and she well knew that what you dream three times will happen. She was doomed to fly and fall and see blood shed. Forebodings darkened her soul and her parents were worried about her. There were even days when she refused food.

Having finished her chocolate she poured tobacco from a little silver box set with a turquois upon a bit of corn husk and with dexterous fingers rolled a cigarette. Where now was that lazy girl?

"Abr-r-rana!" She raised the querulous commanding voice of those who live to be served. *"Vene paca!"*

Abrana, anticipating her want, came running

with a coal from the kitchen fire held between two
splints of fat pine, waved it swiftly into flame
and touched the tip of the cigarette. Lola sank
back upon her pillows, closed her eyes and
assuaged a broken heart with deep puffs that
flowed in blue wisps and clouds from mouth and
nostrils. . . . Life was hard, life was cruel! But
what could one do? Nothing. . . .

She rose lazily when the cigarette had dwindled
to a brown stump and pulled off her night robe,
taking no more notice of the maid than of a cat
or a dog. She became aware of servants only when
they were not where she wanted them.

Abrana, lifting linens from a carved chest of
red wood, was keenly aware of Lola in sidelong
glances. Abrana was squat and bandy-legged with
the flat calves and wide hips of an Indian. She
wore a white *camisa* and a red petticoat that hung
to her knees and nothing else, padding softly on
bare feet, with hair hanging in a thick braid down
her back.

She was adoringly enviously aware of Lola's
long straight legs and of the sweet curve of her
hips and the firm bulge of her breasts that were
like the lift and spread and dwindle of a Guadala-
jara jar. Lola was almost white but without a
trace of pinkness and her hair was coarse black
and shiny as Abrana's own.

Lola was a magnificent vessel but an empty one in Abrana's eyes. She envied Lola her beauty and despised her for being a virgin at eighteen. Abrana was also eighteen and she had known three men and borne one baby. She despised Lola for being a virgin and hoped she would long continue to be one, for she was herself one of the *queridas* of Ambrosio Guiterrez. He had bought her in Sonora for five hundred dollars as a present for Lola and had taken her to his bosom on the way home. Ambrosio made *versos* for Lola and twanged a guitar beneath her window. He sang to Lola of his heart and his soul but he lay with Abrana on warm nights in the orchard and gave her many useful presents.

Pouring water into a silver bowl for her mistress to wash, Abrana prayed silently that Lola might long remain pure.

Lola's ill humor stayed with her all day. Her eyes which were often soft as those of young cattle had all day a smoulder of fire under downdrawn brows. They had the dangerous look of eyes troubled by feelings that rise from the depths of being untouched by thought. Her full lips lay in a crinkled pout. With the kitchen women she was alternately short in her answers and voluble in her curses, reducing them all to frightened silence, almost making them hurry.

"Mary, Mother of God!" she shrilled. "What
have you been doing all day, you lazy Indians?
Do you think you are only here to eat and talk?"

When she called them Indians they knew she
was in her worst humor for it was an insult. All
of them had been born Indians—Navajos, Comanches, Yaquis—all of them had been taken young
in slavery and baptised and given the family name.
All of them now were Christians and to call them
Indians was punishment.

She could not sleep when she retired after dinner because of a dove in a tree behind the house.
Hoowoohoo. . . . Hoo . . . hoo . . . hoo. It
said the same thing mournfully over and over
again and paused each time as though for an
answer that would never come. She felt as though
she could have wrung its neck.

2

Despite her burning restlessness the mighty
routine of her day carried her along its unchanging course. It took her in late afternoon to the *sala*
and sat her down with a needle in her hand to
wait for her father and brothers and any visitors who might come to drink chocolate, gossip
and make a tinkle of music.

The long room was a block of dim coolness for

its three-foot walls kept out the heat and its four little square windows barred with iron and set with mica let in a little light. Before the others came a woman went about on bare feet touching yellow flame to candles in silver sticks. Their light was multiplied in mirrors with gilt frames which had come in but a year before by wagon from St. Louis and were quite the most elegant things in town. Bright pictures of saints and cardinals with folded hands and uprolled eyes of ecstasy hung between them on walls washed ivory white with gypsum and hung to a height of five feet above the floor with dark red calico to keep the whitewash off reclining backs. Red and black Navajo blankets spread divans of rolled mattresses and the floor was softened with a coarse dark woolen carpet and with lambswool rugs washed fleecy white. A tiny shrine where a wooden Jesus drooped on his cross under a silk-purple canopy filled one corner of the room. In another a fireplace was banked for summer with cedar boughs that mingled their odor with smoke of cigarettes.

Lola sewed, bending low to her work, hiding a face she knew was sullen. Her mother leaned a jelly-soft bulk of aged indolence against the wall and lifted a cigarette to her lips with a fat but still pretty hand heavy and helpless with gold and silver. She listened with a weak soft remembering smile to the voice of Ambrosio Guiterrez wooing her daughter with his endless *versos*, squatting on his heels with his back against the wall, strumming and singing softly in effortless monotone like a cricket or a locust.

Ambrosio was never weary of making and singing *versos* and she was never weary of listening to them for they took her back to a time when she had been slim and in love with her husband and to a later time when she had been less slim but still tempting and in love with a priest and a gringo and . . . so many others. . . . It was all so long ago and she was now so fat and life was so sad. . . . The *versos* of Ambrosio brought back all she chose to remember of a long and amorous past. . . .

> Your love to me is water in a deep well.
>   I try with all my might to draw it out.
> My love to you is water in a river
>   That always flows and never knows a drought.

Ambrosio was a loving collector of *versos*. The country was full of them. Everyone made them and sang them. Some were centuries old and had come from Spain and some were made yesterday but they were all alike in the singsong of their

meter, in the sweet sadness and decorum of their
feeling, with here and there a flash of rebellious
humor. Ambrosio liked best the sad ones. He
had chosen for today a lot that expressed the soul
of love denied, patient and yearning.

> They say you are like a flower
> And I say it must be true,
> For though you give your love to none
> All who can see love you.

Forgetting himself and his art for a moment
he let his eyes rest upon his beloved. Her face
was turned away but light fell on the full round
strength of her bent neck, on the lovely play of
muscle in her bare forearm as she sewed and on
a white ankle that a man could have ringed with
his thumb and finger.

So much he could see and all the rest he could
imagine for he knew and loved the bodies of
women and he had never seen a more tempting
one than hers.

He sang of her eyes and her hair and of souls
and hearts for these were the proper and ancient
subjects of song, and he dreamed of the smooth
curve of her hips, the soft pillow of her bosom
and the white latitudes of her belly.

She was like a flower and a singing bird. Her

eyes were wells of mystery and her hair was a cloud. These things he sang for they were the trite and proper subjects of song.

She was like a beautiful colt in a pasture, untouched, unbroken. One longed to feel the spring of her haunches, the quiver and surge of her unconquered flesh.

He could not sing these things but he could think them with a sweetness of anticipation that was increased by modest delay.

Ambrosio was a lover of woman flesh and horse flesh. Women and horses were the delight of his life and they were much alike to him.

The spirit of Ambrosio was passionate but it was not urgent for all things he craved came to him easily.

Leisure he craved and he took it in long lazy hours, sitting on his heels in the shade with his back against the wall, ruminating vaguely upon the pleasant taste of life in a healthy mouth. He did not shirk trouble and work but neither did he hunt them. Daily he rode to the *ranchos* of his father and told peons what to do, riding lordly among them on his pacing sorrel mare. Her gait was a dance and her coat shone like a copper kettle from the hand of a slave. Her barrel was round as the trunk of a tree and her neck arched sweetly as she fought the great Spanish bit in play. When it came his turn Ambrosio took charge of the pack mule train that went from Taos every spring to join the *conducta* below Socorro. Hundreds of pack mules went from New Mexico to Sonora and traded woolen goods for chocolate, coffee, oranges, silk and lace. Ambrosio was a commander who rode a horse at the head of a column and sat by a fire at night while a boy brought him supper and a coal for his cigarette. When Indians attacked Ambrosio charged them in a sudden fury and he had killed an Apache single-handed with a knife. Ambrosio was brave but he was lazy. He never followed them up. . . . In the fall he always went West to the staked plains on a buffalo hunt for blood and excitement were two things his spirit craved. A roan stallion he kept for nothing but buffalo hunting and when the dust of the running herd was before them he and the stallion were one in lust of action. Riding a light saddle, bareheaded, he darted into the thick of the herd. A gun he scorned to use. Guns were for gringos. A lance rested in the hollow of his right arm. His gripping knees steered his flying stallion. He drove the ten-inch blade straight to the heart and whipped it out again—if ever it stuck he might go down among pounding hooves. Peons came after him to butcher his kill, to care for his horse

—he was a lord of slaughter. . . . Gayety his spirit craved and he knew it in *bailes* and fandangos. Dressed in purple velvet trimmed with silver braid, his flaring trousers slit to show his white linen drawers, he waltzed nimbly half the night. Full of music, wine and desire he wandered about the town with his fellows, twanging and singing under windows until he found a pillow to share. . . . For he craved love and it was never denied him. The bodies of slave women were his for the taking and among the bored wives of his friends he carried on complicated and dangerous intrigues with a knife in his belt, always ready to fight and to die if need be. He sinned much and for the most part pleasantly and every week he muttered in confessional the words that brought him absolution and smoothed his path to paradise.

Only the unmarried daughters of the first families were denied him except in marriage and he had chosen the most beautiful of these to be his wife. The wedding had been arranged and all in due course it would happen and delay was not without a sweetness of its own. There was a time for all things and for the taking of any woman a perfect ripe moment to be patiently awaited. . . . In the spirit of Ambrosio was nothing urgent.

That was why Lola felt like pulling his ears.

Her soul and body craved something far more compelling than he could supply. She was bored with his repining ditties and she was tired of looking at his handsome Spanish profile and his shiny black hair. Squatting there on his purple hams, as he had squatted most of the time for months, he reminded her of a tomcat watching a tabby with the endless subtle patience that tomcats have, uttering now and then a yearning meow, roaming widely between times. . . .

> Though you see me with other women
> Do not blush as you pass me by.
> Many go to the fair to look
> Who do not stay to buy.

It was an old *verso* and they nearly all sang it sooner or later. It struck her today as nothing less than a taunt. Ambrosio was free to roam while she was bound within four walls. When she went abroad it was in a coach with her mother. And it would be the same when she was married except that she might take lovers after her husband began to be tired of her, provided he was complacent. If he was not he might punish her in many ways. He might even cut off her ears as old Pedro Sanchez had done with his young wife. Sanchez was a brute, to be sure, but he went unpunished. No man ever lost his ears. . . .

In her mother sitting before her she saw the image of her destiny—to grow fat on idleness, chocolate and wine and sad on neglect. She loved her mother but today she also hated her.

"If you see me with other women." If she hadn't seen him with other women it was because she never had a chance to see anything. A *verso* she remembered leapt to her lips almost before she knew it.

> Your love is like a little dog
> That runs whoever calls.
> My love is like a heavy stone
> That stays just where it falls.

Ambrosio was silent a moment, and then rose and stalked stiffly across the room, standing with his back to her.

He was hurt and insulted and her mother was shocked, speechless at first. Her face slowly deepened into a frowning flush of anger. Then with sudden unexpected agility she sprang up, darted across the room and gave her daughter a sharp slap.

"*Tontita!*" she yelped. "You keep a good man waiting a year after the bans are out and everything is arranged and then you boast about your love. Your love! There is no love in you!"

She began to snuffle, recovered her dignity with

an effort and went back to her place, sitting very straight and ladylike with her small ornamental hands upon her huge maternal hips and her nose elevated at an angle that stretched the folds of her double chin. Her long black earrings trembled with rage. Lola's weepings and nightmares had irritated her for a long time and this was more than she could stand.

Lola's face was dark with rage too, but she did not look up or say a word. One did not reply to a parent any more than to a priest. Parents were sacred.

3

When Don Solomon Salazar came in they all stopped talking and smoking. They waited his pleasure. In this house he the father was God. He had the majesty of a God, tall, erect and dignified with the human mystery of his mouth hidden behind fierce white mustachios. His nose commanded and his eyes defied. His belly bulged with many years of good living. He was dressed in leather but his wealth supported his dignity with a blue serape worth two hundred dollars and a towering black and silver sombrero. A long white scar crossed his cheek from ear to nose.

It was one of many scars that were livid on the

pale polished leather of his aging skin and bloody
still in his aging memory. He was a walking record of Indian battles—whooping, yelling battles
of terrific dust and noise, of soul-satisfying excitement—battles fought with arrows, lances,
muskets, knives and swords, battles of great
glory and little blood. He fought them over end-
lessly in words while his household listened in
drowsy respectful obedience as they listened to
the priest chanting Latin. He liked to begin more
than half a century before when the Comanches
wiped out the first settlement of Taos and galloped away to the mountains with screaming
Spanish women in their arms and Spanish scalps
at their belts. A few survivors got to Mexico City
and these returned and built the walled town.
When the Comanches came again they were ready
for them. Don Solomon's father was among those
who built the town so the Don knew all about
that mighty battle. The Comanches were beaten
—they were all but annihilated. How many were
killed? God knows, but the slaughter was awful.
Dead Comanches littered the valley and blood ran
ankle deep in the roads and they came back to the
town with cartloads of scalps and plunder. . . .

Never after that had wild Indians attacked the
town but all through the youth of Don Solomon
life had been a long series of skirmishes with

Indians who came to raid the herds. Don Solomon had killed Comanches, Apaches and Navajos. He had been shot with arrows in fourteen places, carried a bullet in his left leg and had three knife scars, including one on the back of his neck made by an Apache who tried to scalp him while he lay stunned. The prick of the knife brought him to. He strangled the Apache and scalped him with his own knife. It was his favorite story. His great yellow hands worked when he told it. He could still crumple a silver plate between them.

Well, all that was a long time ago. The Indians were still bad, to be sure, but they seldom raided the principal settlements of New Mexico. Along the Rio Grande from Taos to El Paso the Mexican power sat firm, crops were growing, sheep herds were multiplying into tens of thousands, young men were getting fat and lazy with nothing to fight, devoting their time to cock-pits, monte and the girls. Don Solomon was disgusted with the younger generation. The girls were as bad as the boys. The way they flirted with the gringos! It was revolting. And the gringos were coming more every year with their wagonloads of cheap goods from St. Louis, taking all the money out of the country. They trapped beaver in all the Mexican streams against the Mexican law, bribed the *alcalde* right here in Taos and sold their stolen peltries for Mexican dollars! Then they gave *bailes,* got drunk and made free with the women. . . . Let some gringo lay a finger on his wife or daughter! . . . But the terrible part of it was the women seemed to like them.

And the government? There wasn't any government! Ever since the revolution Mexico City had been a puddle of corruption and in Santa Fe the upstart Armijo, who began life stealing sheep, sat in the governor's palace, looted the treasury to buy Indian girls and sold guns to the Apaches.

For his services against the Indians the government had granted Don Solomon a great tract of land across the mountains. He was to establish there a colony as a bulwark against the gringos and the wild Indians of the prairies. . . . He might as well have tried to colonize the moon. Nobody wanted to go. He was too old himself and young men had no courage any more. . . . What could a man do? Don Solomon rode his acres, drank his wine, cursed man and trusted God.

Now he sat serenely chatting among his family and friends. He told his wife the lambing was good this year and that his herders had killed a wolf and the chile crop was an inch above the ground. He clapped his hands and two Indian girls brought silver pitchers of thick chocolate, silver cups and plates heaped with hot sweet cakes. They all ate, dipping their cakes into thick brown dripping chocolate, munching and talking. Warmed and comforted he stretched his legs, rolled a cigarette and called for a light, graciously bade Ambrosio to smoke—which the younger would never have done without permission. . . . It was an evil and a changing world but here in his thick-walled house were peace and order he had created.

Suddenly they all stopped eating and listened. From the plaza came faintly to their ears a growing rumpus. Dogs barked, a man shouted. Then an Indian chant—a chant not of peaceful pueblos but of wild Indians, riding. "Hai, hai, hai! Haiyai, haiyai, haiyai!"

"Bang!" went a gun. A man shouted.

"Eeowgh! yough!" It was the shrill yell of Apaches!

Don Solomon got to his feet with an agility that he thought he had lost forever. He hurried out and across the *placita,* followed by all the others. The old *portero,* Juan Garcia, who had been with the family twenty years, had opened the double doors a crack and was looking out. He turned to meet them.

"Indios?" Don Solomon demanded, incredulous but eager.

Juan spread his hands and wrinkled his nose. "Gringos!" he snorted in disgust. *"Indios blancos!"*

The Don looked out and saw a band of trappers riding into the plaza with a great dust and thunder of hooves, yelling like Indians as they always did when drunk. One of them had shot his pistol into the air.

Don Solomon, disgusted, turned away. He did not want to see gringos. They had no place in the completed pattern of his life. He snorted and went back to his chocolate and his cigarette. . . . A gringo was something he could neither fight nor love.

Peering through the door opened a crack, with her *reboso* drawn up to hide all but her eyes, Lola watched mountain men ride by. Childlike she sorted them and picked one—a tall lean young man with sunbleached hair blowing wild from under his hat, bleached eyebrows showing like scars against the deep red of his face, eyes bright blue, alert and roaming—she sorted them and picked that one for hers. . . .

He was a strange man from far away, a brave man who went up and down the earth alone with a gun in his hands and fought for his life. He was a wild man, hard to catch and hard to hold, a man uncomforted who slept alone on the hard ground

—a man aching with need of all a woman had to give.

He was dirty, to be sure, but he could be washed and his skin would be so white and his hair so golden.

She would have liked to run out and bid them all come in and give them chocolate and cake. *Pobercitos!* They never had chocolate and cake. . . .

O sweetness she would like to give where sweetness so was needed!

CHAPTER FOUR

I

AM LASH bought him a purple calico shirt, a new clean pair of buckskin pants, tight-fitting, with full fringes, and a pair of Apache moccasins. They had hard cowhide soles with turned up toes and yellow buckskin uppers trimmed with blue beads. He bought him a new black hat with a flat crown and a wide brim and a red silk handkerchief for his neck.

He and Gullion rode out to the hot spring for a bath. Rube Thatcher wouldn't go. He never bathed because it gave him rheumatism and his girling days were over. He was already deep in liquor and in a game of sevenup, squatting with three others around a red blanket littered with silver dollars.

The hot spring filled a square basin of masonry big as a room. The Spaniards had rocked it up long ago and they had done a good job. Water bubbled up through white sand in the bottom and filled the basin with clear pale steaming green. Three Mexican women in red skirts with bare arms were finishing a wash beside it, beating clothes on rocks, soaping them with *amole* roots, spreading them all over half an acre of grass, while their men sat back and smoked and their children paddled in the outlet. When they saw gringos with rifles coming the women gathered up their stuff and started to go, looking back over their shoulders, but Sam Lash told them in Spanish not to hurry and he and Gullion sat down with the men, gave them tobacco and chatted. It was not hard to make friends with poor *pelados* like these. The less a greaser had the friendlier he was. Sam Lash set out to tame the wild brown children with some sugar, luring them close with held-out sweets until he had a circle of chewing, slobbering little greasers around him and was calling them all by their first names. Then an old woman lifted a pot off the fire and brought out a pile of tortillas, a round yellow cheese of goat milk that sliced bone white and a bowl of honey, and they all had to eat. They rolled up tortillas into cups and plunged them into the pot and brought them up dripping full of brown beans, mutton and chile. The Mexicans did it skillfully, and politely refused to look at the mountain men who got it all over their faces and

[71]

fingers and had to lick themselves clean after every mouthful. After the Mexicans were gone with many *adioses* the two lay for an hour in the sun, too full to bathe, lazy as fed cats. Gullion went to sleep as he always did when he was safe and full. Lash lay with his eyes closed seeing the *baile* that night and himself in his purple shirt showing up like a huckleberry in a bowl of milk, wrangling a pretty girl all over the floor.

They eased themselves into stinging hot water an inch at a time, uncertain whether it was agony or delight, until they were in to their necks, and then they lolled in voluptuous unaccustomed comfort.

Reluctantly Lash at last stood up in the sun to dry astonished at his own whiteness, feeling weak and tame. Gullion, squat and bowlegged, still crouched like a big brown muscular frog in a corner. He slowly submerged himself hair and all and came up blowing.

"Good-by nits!" he said, "and no hard feelin's. I got 'em in a Snake lodge on the Yellowstone and this is where I leave 'em."

He viewed Sam Lash with a sardonic envious eye.

"Ain't you a pretty thing!" he taunted. "White as a peeled onion. . . . If them Mexican gals get hold of you they never will let you go."

"Lots of gals has gotten hold of me," said Lash complacently. "And I'm still goin'."

Gullion scrambled out on the rock lip of the basin, gasping.

"I'm limp as a dead snake," he complained. "Injuns know better than we do. They never go in a hot spring. They know it makes 'm weak."

"That ain't why," said Lash contemptuously. "They're skeert. Hot springs is all full of devils to them. A grizzly ba'ar 'll go forty miles to waller in a hot spring and there ain't nothing weak about him."

"Yo're too goddam smart to live," Gullion opined.

2

All diked up in his purple shirt and his red handkerchief Sam Lash went to the padre's house with a package under his arm. It contained a prime squaw-tanned bobcat skin, mottled black and yellow, full-furred and silky to touch. He knew all greasers like bobcat skins. They wear them under their shirts in cold weather to keep the rheumatism out of their backs.

The padre remembered him too and was tickled. He praised the skin and said *"muchas*

gracias," about a dozen times and then "Come in.
My house is yours." He sat Lash down at a table
and a girl brought in a bottle of El Paso wine that
Sam reckoned must have been twenty years old,
it was so warm and gentle in the throat.

They drank and looked at each other, uneasy
friends from far apart. The padre was a young
man, not much older than Lash, lean and limber,
with an eager curious eye. When Sam Lash got up
to leave the padre asked him where he was going
from Taos and Lash said he was going in June to
join a bunch at the Rayado bound for the South.
The padre wished him a safe journey and then
he said:

"Do you ever pray to God, my son?"

Sam Lash said he didn't and the priest asked
him why.

"Well. . . . when I need help I need it so bad
I ain't got no time to pray. . . ."

The padre laughed a little.

"I will pray for you, my son," he said.

He plumped himself down on his knees and
covered his face and stayed that way for what
seemed a long time to Sam.

Sam was uncomfortable standing there looking
down upon the padre's bent neck, listening to his
mumble of supplication. He felt like telling the
padre he was much obliged but not to bother be-

cause he had gotten along this far without a God and probably would go on well enough the same way. He had never taken any stock in any kind of magic. He had never paid Indian medicine men to tell him where his luck lay as many a mountain man did. He had never smoked a pipe beside a sacred spring like Black Harris did. . . . But he couldn't bring himself to interrupt and the longer the padre prayed the more uncomfortable he felt. . . . He was immensely relieved when the padre stood up smiling and held out his hand and looked and talked like a man again.

"God will bless you, my son!"

The padre said it as though it was a sure thing and Sam went out of there stepping light and high. He didn't believe in any kind of magic but no one had ever before gone down on his knees for Sam Lash and it made him feel suddenly as though he was some punkins.

CHAPTER FIVE

I

 HE dance got started slowly as dances always do. An old man on a white mule had ridden round the town ringing a bell. That was an invitation to all and all would come. Some said they wouldn't go to a gringo's *baile* but when they heard a fiddle they would change their minds. Where a fiddle played and a keg was open and a floor was rubbed with candle grease, there you would find the town.

Women came first and banked the benches around the whitewashed walls with bright colors. Here were humble red woolen skirts and proud flowered skirts of imported stuffs, *camisas* of plain cotton and *camisas* of embroidered silk trimmed with heavy laces from Mexico City. Here were bare legs and legs in silk stockings. For all kinds of women came to a *baile* and each wore the best she had. Each made gaudy play with her best mantilla which draped her arms and shoulders, hid her giggles and emphasized her eyes. Each wore all her gold and silver whether it was a single bracelet or enough of them to make her arms heavy, and almost every woman wore a heavy cross of silver or gold riding gently like an anchored boat upon the brown swell of her bosom.

Old women in voluminous black shawls were there early, taking the best seats, nursing tiny yellow cigarettes between withered lips, whispering wise secret words. Women with babies did not stay home but laid sleeping bundles on the floor beside them or quieted squalling ones with modestly naked breasts.

Candles all around the room made a rich uncertain light, leaving furrows of shadow between low heavy rafters.

Men began to gather in the doorway, mostly Mexicans in their best flaring pants and short braided jackets with black hair slick as gun barrels. They did not go in or sit down but stood and leaned, whispered and joked, staring at rows of tittering preening restless girls.

Chabonard, six feet three, master of ceremonies for the mountain men, elbowed and towered through the crowd in the doorway, splendid in a red shirt, with black hair to his shoulders, making way for an old man who bore a cask on his

back. They set it up at the other end of the room,
tapped it and ranged it round with gourd cups.
Here was liquor enough to make the whole crowd
drunk—or if it wasn't more would come. When
mountain men gave a *baile* they did it right.

Baulin, the French fiddler, took his place on a
platform and played. He played alone for he
would play no other way and his music was the
best in the country. He was a small dark shrivelled man and wore a long-tailed maroon coat
with a badly rubbed black velvet collar and a pair
of tight checkerboard pants. On the floor beside
him he set a beaver hat as big as a bucket. His
was the only costume of its kind in town and
Baulin had brought it with him from St. Louis
long ago.

He took his seat frowning heavily and looking
at no one. For a while he sat playing morosely to
himself—wailing bits of this and that mostly
from Mozart. When they brought in the liquor
he paused and snapped his fingers. A boy brought
him a cup of white whiskey. He took it down
neat and easy as if it had been water, cuddled his
fiddle tenderly and played to himself a little more,
rocking in his seat. Then he stood up, looked
around the room for the first time, scornfully,
and with sudden power and spirit played a waltz
that stirred the crowd like wind in leaves,

brought men and girls together whirling and hopping.

2

Lash and Gullion came to the door and looked
in. Only about half the crowd was dancing. A
long row of hopeful girls waited their choice. For
at a *baile* you need no introduction. All you need
is confidence that the girl you want will like your
looks and that you are a better man than her
escort.

Gullion was all for love and battle.

"Come on!" he said. "Here's gals and to
spare."

Lash hung back.

"Aw hell," he said. "I don't want to dance.
Let's go get a drink."

They went to the *cantina* across the street and
each drank a white whiskey with a sudden gulp,
which was the only good way to get it down. Sam
Lash stood fingering his cup and looking at nothing. Gullion was restless.

"Come on!" he said. "Can't you hear that fiddle? This hoss is ra'arin to go."

They went back to the door and looked in
again and again Sam Lash held back. He saw
nothing he wanted. A year before he would have

grabbed the girl that was handiest, but now he was looking for something he couldn't see.

"What in hell's the matter with you?" Gullion demanded. "I believe yo're scared o' them women."

"I ain't scared o' nothin'," Sam Lash said. "What I want 's another drink."

They went across the street and had it and then Gullion went into the hall, leaving Sam still stuck in the door. Gullion picked out a barelegged red-skirted girl and led her onto the floor.

Gullion couldn't waltz any more than an Indian. He danced only mountain man style and that was Indian style adapted somewhat clumsily to ballroom purposes. He got an under hold on his senorita with both arms and then did a shuffle-and-pause like a Comanche going round a scalp pole, chanting as he went. When he got to the end of the floor he lifted his partner and swung her with a whoop. She grinned over his shoulder and dodged his moccasins with nimble feet.

Mountain men were filling the floor now and they danced almost as many different ways as there were men. Some of them could waltz a little but none of them had the hopping agility of the Mexicans and most threw in a few shuffles and grunts they had learned from the Indians.

Greasers were crowded frowning to the walls and not a girl would dance with one if she could get a mountain man. It was always that way. Mexican women would rather have gringos step on their toes than be whirled skillfully by their own kind of men. . . . Mixed *bailes* always moved surely toward trouble.

Sam Lash went back across the street, had a third drink and a fourth—then suddenly knew his pan was primed. He was bound to dance now if he had to dance alone. He got to the door of the hall just as Baulin started to fiddle and the floor was almost empty. He bounced up in the air and cracked his heels and lit doing his Missouri breakdown—a sure sign he was feeling his liquor. Mountain men patted and stamped to keep him time and egged him on, girls laughed at him and greasers looked black disgust at his bad manners.

He stopped and stood in the middle of the floor, owning it for a minute.

"Gimme a gal!" he shouted. "I want to dance. . . ."

They all laughed. . . . And then a girl came forward.

He hadn't really expected any and certainly not such a one as this. For she was a *rico*, gorgeous in a white skirt worked with red and yellow flowers, a silk bodice trimmed with lace and a red and black mantilla over one shoulder. A red paper rose was stuck in her heavy black hair behind one ear.

As she left her seat an old woman beside her made a scandalized grab to stop her but it was too late. Eyes and teeth shining with excitement she waltzed up to Sam Lash and held out bare silver-bound arms to him.

Sam didn't rise to her any too lively. He stood staring at her for a minute open-mouthed. She seemed to take all the caper out of him.

He felt as though someone had given him a basket of eggs to carry. He was used to strong-flavored squaws that craved to be handled rough and to the common Mexican women that were not much different. This girl was so slick and dainty and sweet-smelling that he was almost afraid to take hold of her. He was afraid his great hot hands would muss her up. He was glad he had washed himself and sorry he had drunk so much because he was sweating like a nigger. His legs had gone stiff under him. He was a good dancer but he couldn't dance good now. . . .

She was the tallest woman ever he had squared up against since he left Kentucky. Most of them in these parts were built low and wide. They hit him about the middle and hung heavy on his arm.

But this child was right up with him where he lived.

Generally a woman at a *baile* was only something to swing but this one filled his eye with her strange white softness come close as he took her gingerly in his arms and began to dance. His mouth was right beside her ear but he couldn't find a word to say.

"Don't you speak Spanish, sir?" she asked him softly.

"Yes, miss, I speak it very well," he answered like a little boy to a school teacher and felt foolish.

"Then why don't you talk to me?" she asked and he knew she was making fun of him and that made him feel better.

"You are so pretty," he told her. "I can only look at you."

It was easy to say things like that in Spanish.

"Then perhaps I had better go back and sit down," she suggested. "You could see me better. . . .

Sam tightened his hold on her just a little.

"I would as soon have my hand cut off!"

Spanish was made for that kind of patter but he felt as though he meant it.

Talking he began to forget his feet and find his joints. He was moving easy now and she filled his

[83]

arms like honey in the mouth, sweet soft and everywhere.

Music stopped and he stood before her as she took her seat, smiling up at him, beside the old woman who scowled at him. He knew she had gone against her family to dance with him, knew she had picked him out of the crowd and it made him feel taller to know it.

He went outside and walked around a little but he was soon back in the doorway. He couldn't keep his eyes off her.

She welcomed his stare as Spanish women always do, touching a self-conscious hand to her hair, shifting her shawl, spilling a bit of a look his way but never meeting his eager eye.

He felt uncomfortably held. . . . Women often caught his eye and held him that way, made him feel picketed. But generally he stared himself free. He found something in most of them he didn't like.

So he stood staring at her, looking for what might free him, and she sat preening triumphant under his eye. For she looked perfect to him as birds and flowers are perfect.

Her duenna began to scold her, waving fat eloquent hands heavy with rings. A young Mexican in purple velvet walked up and joined the confab and then another older woman came and they hid her in a chattering, gesticulating group. As always with Mexicans everything was a family affair. . . .

He went outdoors and dodging friends walked alone where wind cooled his hot face. He walked about swinging his arms and frowning.

"Phew!" he blew. "I'm a fool for women," he told himself aloud. He swept a bewildered hand across his eyes as though to wipe away webs of illusion.

Every once in a while he went back and looked in the door but always she was dancing and generally with the young Mexican in the purple suit. It looked like a plan to keep him away from her and he wasn't surprised. Rich Mexicans were all against gringos.

He kept going away and coming back restlessly, not wanting to dance with any other, watching his chance.

Every time he looked in at the *baile* it was going stronger as the white whiskey ebbed in the keg. The floor was jammed and the air was full of smoke. Already he had seen several spats between gringo and greaser over girls and each time a white man had pushed a brown one off the floor. So far nobody had struck a blow or flashed a knife but he could see trouble coming. It was a poor *baile* that didn't start a fight.

At last he saw her left alone and made straight for her. The way she came up smiling to his arms made him warm and swell inside. They hadn't turned her against him—that was sure. . . .

"How are you called, sir?" she enquired politely in the Spanish idiom.

"Sam Lash," he said. "And you?"

"I am Lola Salazar," she said and she rolled the last name proudly.

"Lola Salazar," he said solemnly. "If ever you want a fool gringo here is one you can have."

"Thank you, sir."

Her words were demure and decorous and as she said them she leaned back against his arm and pressed herself for a moment, boldly, tenderly against him.

As she did it he could see the blood climb her bare neck and his own rose thundering in his ears. . . .

3

Gullion was arguing noisily with a slick slim little Mexican over the red-skirted girl Gullion had been dancing with most of the evening. The crowds whirled and parted around them. The girl stood on one foot looking modestly down while the white man blustered and the dark one stood his ground, insisting with a politeness that covered a hatred old and over-ripe. Gullion ended the argument by flattening a great hand against the Mexican's expostulating mouth, knocking him down and away with a long shove.

"Off the floor, you goddam greaser," he roared. "You can't shine here. . . ."

The Mexican bounced to his feet neatly plucking out a hidden blade as he rose and made a wild pass at Gullion, slitting his shirt but getting no blood. Before he could recover Gullion's left fist sent him sprawling. He was up almost before he landed and the two crouched face to face on a widening floor. Gullion had drawn a hunting knife with a fourteen-inch blade. His drunken fighting rage was on him now. The fingers of his left hand worked and his lips writhed over his teeth.

Chabonard signalled to Lash and they ran between the two. Lash got the Mexican with both arms and held him pinioned but Gullion dodged Chabonard. Not to be denied his blood he sprang like a wild cat and made a crossing slash at the Mexican. Lash snatched his man away but the point of the blade nicked his neck and blood ran down his shirt.

Chabonard had Gullion now and dragged him away writhing and blubbering.

"Lemmego, lemmego!" he begged. "I'll cut the

son of a bitch in two. . . . I'll have his guts by
God!"

The floor had cleared by now, women crowding
back against the walls screaming, covering faces
with hands and peering between fingers. Mexicans
were massing in the doorway in a muttering crowd
and more seemed to come from outside. Fifty
hidden blades came flashing to light.

Some were trying to hold the crowd back and
make peace and some were egging it on.
Two Mexicans came to take their injured fellow
away from Lash. He let them have him, drew his
knife and went over to the other end of the room
where mountain men had gathered about Gullion
and Chabonard near the musician's platform. . . . Baulin, fiddle and all, had crawled
under it.

Some among the Mexicans were still trying to
hold the mob back but anybody could see it was going to be war. There were fifty greasers at one end
of the room and eleven mountain men at the other
and greasers loved that kind of a break. Chabonard jumped up on the platform and waved his
arm.

"Up here, boys!" he shouted. "Hell's about to
pop!"

They all scrambled up after him with drawn
knives. Some stripped off their shirts and wrapped

their left arms for guards. Most of them were grinning.

Chabonard, a man of resource, climbed onto a heavy pine table that stood at the back of the stage, jumped up and down with all his weight and the power of his legs, smashing it to pieces. Swiftly he wrenched loose legs and put them into the hands of his fellows.

The mob milled and wavered like cattle before a storm, then charged with a yell.

Women went screaming out the door. Somebody began knocking candles out and the forces collided in a dim light that presently became solid darkness filled with curses in two languages, grunts, yells and the scrape and thud of fighting feet.

Sam Lash with a table leg in one hand and a knife in the other battered madly at a surging front of charging men more felt than seen. Sometimes his club thudded heavily on flesh and sometimes it swung through empty air. Someone got under his guard grabbed his ankle and threw him heavily backward. Lying flat he kicked a man in the face, knocking him off the platform, and got up again.

Clubs won the battle. Not a Mexican could get a foothold on the platform. Leaders went down with cracked heads and followers tripped over

them in the dark. It was a mob against an organi-
zation.

The Mexicans fell back, many of them running
from the door. The mountain men charged with
a yell and drove them all out into the street. . . .
The crowd scattered. . . .

4

The rest were all gone but Sam Lash still hung
around the door of the deserted hall. He was
bruised and felt himself carefully all over in the
dark but found little blood and no broken bones.

He knew it wasn't safe for a gringo to go alone
in the night now. Probably no one was killed or
even badly cut but there were a lot of sore Mexican heads in town. . . . Looking around he
found a tall sombrero some Mexican had left behind in his hurry. He threw away his own hat and
put on the tall one. In the dark he was as good a
greaser as any.

Restless and aimless he prowled through narrow lanes between mud walls. Shadowy curs
yapped at his heels. Yellow lights looked at him
through little bar-striped windows. Under one of
them a greaser tinkled a guitar and sang in a low
voice. From a black patch of shadow Sam watched
and saw the light go out and bare arms and a

face appear—saw lovers kiss and turned away hating them.

He couldn't tinkle a guitar. He couldn't sing. He didn't even know where she lived.

What he wanted was somewhere behind thick walls and barred windows, protected from him by an ancient hatred. . . . But he could see her in the dark and touch her though she wasn't there. The ghost of her hand was in his hand and he still burned from the sudden willing pressure of her flesh.

CHAPTER SIX

I

AULIN crawled out from under the platform when he felt sure the room was empty and closed the heavy double doors.

Gropingly he struck light and set a candle on the floor where it wouldn't show.

He brushed the dust off the knees of his checkerboard trousers and adjusted the collar of his coat and his wide black cravat. On his head he poised the pompous burden of his beaver hat. Then he went to the keg, hesitantly eager as a lover to his girl, rocked it gently and heard with brightening eye the splash of liquor.

Filling a gourd cup he sipped it and set it on the platform. Sitting beside it he cuddled his fiddle and softly sadly played. Every few minutes he paused to sip the cup and when it was empty he paused to fill it with trembling careful hands.

At last the keg would give him no more tilt it as he might. He tilted it too far and fell over on the floor with it, got up with difficulty and sat on it, feeling as though he sat on the corpse of his last friend.

Baulin now was drunk and when he was drunk he was sad. For that matter he was often sad when he was sober but in a morose and sometimes in a savage way. Drunk he was gloriously expansively sad. He longed to weep and make sad music and he longed for thousands to listen and weep with him.

Baulin was an artist and therefore all the sorrows of the world entered into his soul when he was sad and drunk.

Baulin did not want to go home because either that fat wench of a Soledad whom he had married in a misguided hour would be waiting for him with her temper up or else some dirty gringo would have the other half of his bed and he would sleep on the kitchen floor.

He did not want to go home because inside of him all the sadness of unrequited love throbbed as a beautiful tune.

He did not want to go home. . . . He wanted to utter the sadness of his soul in perfect music and he wanted lovely women to listen and weep.

Woman was perfect music rendered into flesh. . . . Woman was an ill-tempered animal who could be soothed only by virile exercises difficult for Baulin at any time and impossible when he was drunk.

Baulin did not want to go home. He wanted to fiddle under a window and see a fair hand toss him a rose.

Long ago in St. Louis Baulin had fiddled under a window and a fair hand had tossed him a rose. Moreover he had scaled a porch with an agility which was no longer in his legs and had tasted the sweet rewards of his power. . . . What is memory but a cut that never heals? . . . The result was a wide-hatted man twice his size hunting him with a gun and Baulin taking sudden passage on a wagon bound for the West.

He was a man of art and love but not of battle. Violence he could never face. Therefore Baulin, an artist, was an exile in a savage land where a violinist was a fiddler and his only use to make people dance. He played Cucuracha and Turkey-in-the-straw for his bread while youths and maidens whirled and sweated in each other's arms and for the consolation of his inconsolable spirit he played Mozart to himself when he was drunk and alone.

Leaving his dead friend the keg Baulin fumbled his way to the door and went zig-zagging slowly down the street and into the plaza. He stopped and stood in the middle of it and lifted

[94]

a bitter face to the stars, conscious of himself there as a lone and tragic figure, magnificent in his isolation though unsteady on his legs.

Heavy walls black in shadow shut him in and over them he saw dimly the awful silhouette of endless mountains full of lions, bears and wild men who lived by killing.

The mountains of the blood of Christ they called them because they glowed so red when the sun set.

Red they glowed when the sun set as though all the blood of men and beasts who had died among them glistened wet on the teeth of their pointed peaks.

Black they were now and cold stars and black mountains chilled and shrivelled his spirit.

Not a foot or a voice stirred in the sleeping village. Baulin felt as lonely as the last man on a dying planet.

He should have lived soft in the lap of a shining singing city where the breasts of women budded sweetly from the bodices of perfect gowns under the yellow eyes of many candles.

Why had he not run East instead of West? What malign God had planted him here—a seed in a soil that could not nourish it?

He was a wasted thing for his youth was over but his spirit was unconquered. He was full of the

[95]

white fire of inspiration and corn whiskey. . . .
He would play.

He took off his hat and set it on the ground
beside him, straightened his cravat, threw back
his head, closed his eyes and played.

His closed eyes saw the darkness punctured
with faces. He felt it pregnant with the warmth
of human response. . . .

Through to the end he played, nourishing a
vision on a tune—then opened his bewildered
eyes on the silence and solitude of reality.

A dog up an alley answered his music with a
long doleful howl and a coyote in the foothills
took up the cry in a thin weird voice—the voice
of a subhuman world, savage and uncomprehend-
ing.

Baulin stood a moment blinking away his
dream. Then he picked up his hat and staggered
on his way, drooping under the burden of his
pity for himself.

Led by habit he trudged uncertainly up the road
to his home. . . . But he could not go home.
Then where could he go? A man has to go somewhere. . . .

He saw a dim light in a window and this signal of human presence stopped his feet and held
his eyes. Somewhere in that house was another
awake and perhaps as lonely and miserable as he.

Perhaps some girl had brought home from the dance a heart too full or too sore for sleep and sat beside a candle. . . . With music he would reach her.

Under the window he stopped and played. Absorbed in his playing he forgot everything else. He escaped again through his fingers. His soul flew wailing away.

He did not hear the window open but he felt the cold splash of water on his bent neck and heard a woman's voice in shrill angry Spanish.

"Run along home, you old drunk. . . . It's time to sleep!"

It had happened before. He ought to have known better. None of the village girls would ever listen to his playing. Music was lost on these brown barbarians except when they could dance. What they wanted under their windows was not an artist but a lusty young buck full of the irreplaceable juices of youth.

As he plodded on sober and damp, mopping the back of his neck, Baulin knew where he was going now. . . . He knew that now his feet would carry him to the graveyard.

He did not know why, but always on his worst nights of misery and liquor when all the living had scorned him he had gone to serenade the dead. More than once he had spent the night among the

tombstones but generally compassionate peons
came and carried him home.

2

In the graveyard white wooden crosses stood
in barren sand over bones buried under many
rocks to keep wolves from digging them up.
Withered flowers hung on a few of the crosses and
there was one grave new dug.

Baulin knew that the air here was full of hover-
ing presences. When younger he had gone around
graveyards, he had crossed himself as he passed
them, had dreaded to see filmy forms arise from
the ground. But he was no longer afraid of death
or of the dead. It was only violence he feared.
One who has failed in art and love belongs more
to the dead than to the living. One who cannot
make the living listen still can play to the unpro-
testing dead. . . . Baulin knelt because his legs
were now very unsteady and played.

He started when a hand fell on his shoulder
from behind.

Terrified, he looked up into the face of a tall
man who had followed him. By the sound of the
man's voice, though he spoke in Spanish, he knew
this was a gringo.

Incredibly the gringo held out a palm containing silver. He, Baulin, was being offered money to play a tune!

And did he know where Lola Salazar lived? Certainly he knew where everybody lived and if he did not know which room, still he knew what part of the house would contain the women.

Could he play a tune under her window? He could play anything anywhere, but the trouble was he had lost the use of his legs. Once he was down, like a cow in a bog, he could not rise again. He tried but it was no use.

Then the gringo knelt and took Baulin upon his back, seized him by both legs, lifted him, carried him away.

O what a mighty man was this! Baulin's head was high in the air. Baulin had acquired the legs of a giant and strode through the town seven feet tall.

Baulin wanted to play a march of triumph, but he had to hold onto the gringo's shirt to keep from falling so he only hummed as they went along, and dogs barked at this composite monster who marched for conquest. . . .

CHAPTER SEVEN

HREE squatted on their heels in the plaza and held pow-wow.

"What I want to know," said old Rube Thatcher, "is why this here outfit don't hit the road. Ain't we all been drunk and got sober again? Ain't this coon lost beaver hoss an' shirt buckin' a greaser monte game? Ain't we all sick of beans and chile and half froze for good red meat? Right now I'd swap a pile of tortillas a mile high for one good humprib. I reckoned this time to keep my dollars in my jeans and pull for the Missouri and set easy what years I got left. I didn't do it and it ain't the first time I missed my chance. But there's more beaver where that come from and this coon feels like travellin'."

Lash drew lines on the ground with a stick and said nothing. Gullion talked for him.

"Sam here's gone squamptious on a Mexican gal and won't pull out without her," he explained. "He wants us to help him get her. After that ruction last night he can't do no business with the family an' I reckon he couldn't anyway. His only chance is to grab her an' go same as young Dick Wooton done in California last fall. . . ."

"Same as many a damn fool's done," said Rube Thatcher, disgusted. "If Sam here craves a woman why don't he buy him a squaw that'll be some good to him an' trail along with him where he goes? What kin a man do with a Mexican woman but set and watch her or go off and leave her? Ef he sticks with her he jest goes greaser himself. Sam here ain't gonna quit the mountains and turn bean-eater, is he? I can understand a man that pulls fer white country and marries a white woman and builds a log house and eats hog an' hominy, because that's what we all come from. I've always figgered to do it sometime myself. . . . I had a gal in Independence once—she's either dead now or a grandmother—and she was as slick a piece as a man could want. Ef I'd had sense enough t' stick by her I'd be settin' on my own stoop right now smokin' a pipe and hearin' pa'tridges whistle in a corn field and smellin' hog jowl and greens a-cookin'. . . . Now that there's something t' eat, lemme tell you, but who the hell wants to burn his mouth on chile the rest of his life. A man had better keep goin' till he gets rubbed out. . . ."

"All that ain't neither here nor there," Gullion objected.

"It's both," said Rube Thatcher with authority. "I ain't lived in these mountains since the Rio Grande was a spring branch fer nothin'. I seen many a good man marry Mexican and I ain't seen one yit that wasn't sorry. Them women breeds like prairie dogs an' jest as careless. They look good when they're young but after they've calved a time or two they swell up like a cow in a truck patch an' you need a wagon to move 'em. They do nothin' but eat and holler like a guinea keet. . . . And all their kids is jest as Mexican as they are. . . . I mind Joe Thomas that was as good a mountain man as ever set a float stick and he went loco over a brown gal in El Paso. Her family hated gringos, so he snatched her up in his saddle and ran to Socorro with her. I seen him there about six years later settin' in a barroom lookin' sad and peaked as a moulted rooster. He looked out the window kind of sorrowful. 'Yander comes five goddam greasers,' he says. 'Who ere they?' somebody asks. 'M' wife and the four kids,' says Joe. . . . Now mind me, Sam Lash, ef you git away with this gal you'll be jest that sad. It'll be the end o' your travels and the start o' your sorrows. . . . Who is the woman, anyway?"

[102]

"Old Solomon Salazar's daughter."

"Phew!" Rube whistled amazement. "That there's worse and more of it. Ef it was some common wench with nothin' to her name but a chile pot and a 'dobe shack it wouldn't be so bad. Her padre'd raise hell for a while but a few hundred dollars would fix him. But these here Salazars are *ricos*. They probably got Indian in 'em same as all the rest, but they think they're fine people and they're proud as hell and won't look at money. They got here first and grabbed all the good land along the crick bottoms. Salazar and Miranda hold a Mexican grant to a lot of country across the mountains too. They own more land than they'll ever see an' more sheep than they ever counted. You can't tell 'em nothin' and they won't look at you when they ride by. A gringo is jest simply something they can't see. . . . I don't believe Sam Lash kin git away with no such gal but ef he does he's unlucky, that's all I got to say. . . . An' s'posin' he does git her, what's he gonna do with her?"

"He kin run her up to Bent's Fort and marry her, can't he?" Gullion argued. "It's been done afore now plenty o' times. . . . No greasers is gonna follow very far North. They're too skeered o' Comanches. . . ."

"He kin marry her after a fashion but it won't

count for no marriage with her folks. . . . An'
after he's married her, then what's he gonna do?
There he'll set with a woman on his hands and
not a dollar to his name . . ."

"He kin go on about his business, and leave her
there, can't he? Bent's is always littered up with
squaws an' such like that's been left there. . . .
He kin meet us on the Rayado and go South with
us and come back, if he's a mind to, before
snow. . . ."

"First off, he's gonna have one hell of a time
gettin' away, and ef he does, when he gits back,
he'll find the gal gone. An' that won't be so bad
fer him neither, only he won't never be able to
show his head around Taos again without trouble,
and it'll be just that much more they'll have agin
all gringos. This is where we trade and every ruction we have makes it harder. You young fellers
went and raised a stink last night at that *baile* and
busted a couple of greasers wide open and it cost
us two hundred dollars to square it with the
alcalde. Now we run off with a gal on top o' that.
It won't do, I'm tellin' ye. . . ."

"O to hell with you!" Gullion was getting mad.
"It's all right fer you to talk that way. You got
ha'ar in yer ears and no more use fer a woman
than a beaver has fer two tails. . . ."

"Another thing I ain't got no use fer," Rube

broke in, rising and towering over them with a
hand on a knife handle, "is a bandy-legged little
son-of-a-bitch that's always fer startin' trouble.
. . . Why in hell are you so hot fer this ruction
anyway? You don't think yo're gonna git the gal,
do you? Yo're jest one o' them locoed galoots
that'd be in the hoosegow ef there was any. You'd
rather start trouble than not, jest to see hell pop.
Yo're the one that started that rib-ticklin' spree
last night, and I knowed you'd do it jest as sure
as you took a drink and went there. You trail
around after Sam Lash like a lost dog and you
ain't never done him no good yit. There he sets
not sayin' a damn word. . . . He knows this here
is a fool trick he's up to. I thought maybe I could
talk sense into him but I see I can't and I'm
done!"

He stood over them, a tower of scorn. He was
their own hard strength looking down upon their
woman-loving softness, despising it. Neither of
them met his eye. Sam Lash looked at the ground.
Gullion turned dark with rage under insult and
his fingers worked but he made no move. He was
afraid of old Rube.

When Rube had gone they got up and mosied
around.

"I reckon you don't want to travel like Rube
says," Gullion hazarded after a while.

Sam shook his head. He could no more travel than if he had been tied to a tree.

After a while they found Chabonard and Gullion told him all about it too. He showed white teeth in a wide grin. He was always ready for that kind of thing.

"Kin you git word to the gal?" he asked Sam. "Kin you git her out in the plaza?"

Sam nodded.

"All right. Jest after sunup tomorrow. We're pulling out then. All you got to do is pick her up and ride. We'll cover you with ten rifles. There won't be no trouble about it—leastways not on the go-off."

CHAPTER EIGHT

I

 HE could not go. She would not go. Her whole life crowded around her and pulled her back.

Walls that had held her ever since she was born would not let her go now.

She was afraid to go but more than she was afraid she was held back by every familiar thing. The dove in the cottonwood tree plead with her to stay and the gaudy picture of the Mother of God that hung on the wall plead with sad eyes and barred the way.

Her memories were a load that weighed her down, too great for her to move. Everything safe and happy came back to her now. She saw herself a little girl romping wild with her brothers through long cool adobe rooms, pestering women at work in the kitchen, waiting eager for the opening of an earthen oven where sweet things were baking, stealing brown sugar from the great dark storeroom, heavy with the smell of dried meat,

[107]

chile, onions and coffee. . . . She went again all in white like a little angel to be received into the arms of the church, to be promised paradise by a parent just and eternal in return for obedience. She heard again solemn voices chanting mysteriously potent words, smelled the scented breath of divine presence, saw sacred candles pointing yellow fingers toward heaven before the lifesize figure of Jesus drooping cadaverous on his cross with blood painted scarlet on his feet and hands and brow—a horrible figure that had become to her a thing as sweet and comforting as her mother's smile. . . . She knelt trembling in her first confession and mumbled to God that she had stuck out her tongue behind her mother's back after a scolding and that she and her little cousin Juan—. Mother of God, how could she say it? . . . And the divine forgiveness descended upon her real and sweet as a kiss, and she went forth pure and good. . . . It was San Geronimo day and she walked in a long procession behind a Virgin Mother made of plaster while men fired off muskets and sang. . . . It was Easter and she saw a crowd of half naked men, marching up a wind-beaten hill, lashing backs that bled for the sins of men as He had bled. . . .

Why came all these days now to plague her and what had they to do with her going? . . . She

was going. . . . She was not going. . . . She
was going to her first dance again in her first
dress that fell below her knees. For the first time
with a tingle that ran to her toes she felt the eyes
and hands of men upon her and she chose Tircio
because he was a golden head among black ones.
When the dance was nearly over two old men
caught her, as was the custom, and carried her
around the hall on a chariot of crossed hands and
would not let her out of chancery until her parents had promised to give a dance in her honor.
. . . After that there were many dances and she
was a good dancer and loved to dance. The
rhythm of all her dances held her now as a thread
she could not break and the hands and arms of
all the men she had danced with were upon
her. . . .

She had not slept until near morning, and then
she dreamed horribly again, for the third time
within a month, of flying and falling and of blood.
That was why she could not put away all these
figures and faces of things she had thought forgotten that came and surrounded her now and
held her in chancery and would not let her go.
. . . And yet hands were upon her pulling her
away too—hands that had reached up out of the
dark to claim her when she went to the window to
send old Baulin home, hands that had come back

next night with a message. . . . And she had promised. . . . But she could not go. That was sure. Everything that belonged to her and everything she belonged to was here. To go was sin and even to think of going was madness. Her father and mother looked at her now with sad suffering eyes. She could not see them frown. She could not hear them scold. If only someone had found out and come to stop her it would be easier, but only patient pleading ghosts of days came to stop her and she could not fight them off. . . .

And yet she had made a bundle and stood ready to go and there was still time. A foolish *verso* kept running through her mind—an old *verso* she had heard:

> I don't want to go
> I don't want to stay
> Nor that you leave me here
> Nor take me away. . . .

She wished her gringo would suddenly burst into the room with his awful gun and his knife and his bright blue fearless eyes and seize her and drag her away and she would not care if he hurt her. She wished her father would come, stern and terrible, and forbid her to go, lock her up, beat her even. . . . She wished to God someone, with more strength of arm and heart than she, would take off her back the unendurable burden of deciding her destiny. . . .

She wished even that Ambrosio would come, not tinkling and singing but with a naked blade to fight for her. She did not belong to Ambrosio but an Ambrosio terrible and resolute might have held her and she wanted something to hold her.

She did not belong to Ambrosio. She belonged to the gringo and solely because his hand upon her had stirred her as had no other. She did not belong to Ambrosio but she belonged to his life. . . . It was not right for her to run away into mountains with a strange wild man. It was right for her to sit and wait and in due course be married with little girls in white walking behind her and a robed priest standing over her as she knelt in the church. It was right for her to live easily in a great house and have many babies and grow fat on chocolate idleness and wine while Ambrosio went in search of youth and slenderness. . . .

It was right that she should stay—but her feet carried her softly out of the room and her eyes were alert for any that might stop her. . . .

2

The plaza this early was almost empty. Doors

were closed and a few plumes of early smoke showed where servants were astir.

Houses laid down long angular shadows on one side of the square and on the other slanting sunlight picked out shining particles of mica in yellow earthen walls. A wood vender trudged behind three gray burros ambling under enormous loads of yellow pitch-pine and an Indian woman walked sedately with a red bundle on her head, her soft-shod feet caressing the earth in careful steps.

Lola had never seen the plaza so empty, so early. She felt as though she had emerged upon a strange new world. She walked with difficulty not daring to turn her head, imagining eyes behind every door and window, expecting to jump at the touch of a hand or the sound of a voice.

She did not believe even now that she was going but her feet carried her to the corner opposite the church and she stood there with weak knees feeling that in another minute she would sit down and weep.

A party of buckskinned men with long rifles across their saddle-bows, driving packmules before them, rode past her and looked at her with the bright hard eyes of the ruthless and alert. Their looks pricked her skin like knives. They stopped on the opposite corner and made jokes and laughed. . . .

Her man came riding a little behind them.

He rode a tall square-built glossy roan that fought the bit. He held his mount to a jog and sat straight and easy in his saddle like a man out for a morning ride.

His eyes were unwavering upon her and as he came closer she could see nothing but the bright devouring excitement of his eyes.

He rode as though he would ride by, then suddenly spun his horse and stooped. . . . She felt his arm about her, felt herself lifted, felt the sudden powerful spring of the horse under spur. . . .

Over his shoulder she saw the wood vender running, heard a shout, saw the others close in across the road, barring the way with rifles ready. . . .

Hooves drummed in her ears, wind tore at her flying hair and her frightened mouth tasted the buckskin of his shirt. . . .

CHAPTER NINE

I

AM LASH made his camp a little way from the others. He picked a flat high place where ground was smooth and cut cedar boughs and built a shelter while she sat on his saddle with her back to a tree and watched.

Never had he built such a big shelter nor such a good one. He made a triangle of small logs laid cattiwampus and against the outside of it he piled cedar boughs thick with sweet-smelling needles.

He roofed over the top the same way, choosing and placing boughs with a nice eye, trying and throwing aside, trying again, making as good a house as any man could make with an axe and an hour of daylight.

He brushed out the inside with a bough and covered the ground with tips of blue spruce which was more than ever he had done for himself. Over them he laid a buffalo robe and over the robe he spread a black and red Navajo chief

[114]

blanket so tightwoven it would hold water. He dug a trench all around the uphill side so that rain would drain off and he hung a saddle blanket to make a door. . . . His reward was that when she went inside she kissed him and didn't look so scared.

He walked up the mountain and sat down and lit a pipe and looked a while at his house with his woman inside and then he went down to where the others sat around a fire and he sat down too.

Several jugs of liquor were going around as always happened the first day out. Some were telling tall stories, some wanted to sing and some wanted to fight.

Gullion was one that had his dander up. He had set a jug of forty-rod over against a tree. He kept marching around the fire, blowing his horn, and every time he reached the jug he stopped and took a long gurgling swig and then went on with his war talk louder than ever. Nobody was paying him much notice yet, but it was clear somebody would have to crawl his frame before the night was over.

He kept telling them all that he was a ring-tailed roarer, that he was a flying wild cat and when he lit the fur flew, that he hadn't had a fight for three days and was getting so wolfy his skin itched.

He was short squat and bandy-legged but light on his feet with wide shoulders and long arms. He worked himself up like a rooster. He flapped his arms, jumped up in the air and cracked his heels. He did a little Blackfoot war dance all by himself and then he did a little strut with his fists working up and down, his back swayed and his behind sticking out.

"I'm on the prowl, boys!" he shouted. "Ef anybody wants to live long let him stay out o' my way!"

Nobody took any notice of him because nobody else felt like fighting just then and they all knew he got that way when he was in liquor. He couldn't live without fighting.

He had just started around the fire for another drink when he spied Sam Lash sitting quiet in a shadow with his elbows on his knees looking hard at the fire.

"Whoopee boys!" he yelled. "Look'ee here what I found! Damned if it ain't the bridegroom hisself settin' here all alone and lookin' sad as a sick chicken. What's the matter, Sam boy? Did she throw you out? Was she too wild to ride?"

They all looked and laughed and that egged Gullion more than a dozen drinks.

"He's skeert of her, boys," he taunted. "Now that he's caught his squaw he don't know what to do with her. . . . Why ain't you with her, boy?"

Sam Lash didn't move but his face turned red as the fire.

"Cut that chin music," he growled. "this child ain't turned nigger yet. . . ."

"You ain't turned nigger?" Gullion bawled. "An' I reckon you think you kin set there and tell me I have. . . . Stop my chin music, is it? Lemme see you stand up and make me stop it, you big long drink o' water, you. Yo're so goddam tall you cain't tell when your feet's cold, but that ain't no odds to me. The higher they are the harder they fall. When I light on you, boy, you'll break in the middle and hit in two places at oncet. Wait till I git a bite hold on you an' we'll see who's turned nigger, goddam my eyes if we don't!"

Sam Lash stood up slowly, his face twisted into a heavy scowl, his fists clenched, his feet wide planted. Gullion capered around him dribbling with eagerness, both arms crooked, his great stubby fingers spread and working. He was not a boxer but a scrouger. It was a hold he hankered after and when he got one he was bad.

"Yo're my meat now, you pretty thing!" he gloated. "When I git done with you your gal won't be able to tell whether yo're comin' or goin'. You won't have no more face than a toadstool.

[117]

. . . You've been gettin' too goddam uppety for a month. Jest because the Mexican gals runs after you, you think yo're a man, and jest because your folks owned a few rickety niggers and a couple o' razor-back hawgs you think yo're too goddam good fer all the rest of us. . . . You wouldn't never of had that gal if I hadn't helped you to git her and now you set there and tell me I'm a nigger. . . . I'll learn you manners, you long-legged son-of-a-bitch. . . ."

At the last word Sam Lash took a quick step forward and drove in with a right swing that started down around his knees. Gullion ducked back like a dog from a mule kick and tried to run in, but he met Sam's left with the side of his head and fell ten feet away. He came right up, spluttering and breathing hard, blood trickling from his ear. He was hard-headed as a mule and could take terrible punishment.

Chabonard tried to stop it but no one would help him. They were all set to see a ruction.

"Game cocks is bound to fight when there's a hen among 'em," old Rube Thatcher decided. "Let 'em fight. It's jest a social ruction. They ain't neither of 'em got no steel on and they bin workin' up to this all winter."

It was the general judgment. Men had a right to fight when a fight didn't interfere with business. The group fell back making a wide half circle. High, red pitch-eating flames lit their eager interested faces.

Gullion pulled off his hat and sailed it into the dark. He peeled his buckskin shirt over his head and threw it on the ground.

"Lay there till I need yuh," he told it.

He showed a hairy chest and arms of enormous knotty muscle. With his shirt off he looked bigger and uglier. Sam Lash seemed slim beside him, a head taller but not as heavy.

Gullion, his mouth shut at last, circled him warily and Sam Lash waited with his knees bent and his hands lifted. Their long shadows crawled and wavered over firelit ground.

Gullion's game was to get a hold and Sam's was to stand off and wallop. It was bulldog against wolf. They both knew that. Each had seen the other fight more than once. . . .

Gullion shuffled forward, stuck out his face and moved his head like a turtle.

"Come on . . . hit me," he challenged. "What's the matter? Are you hamstrung?"

But Lash was too wary to swing. He knew that if he missed and lost his balance he would be down in a minute.

Gullion was not too drunk to make a good fight but he was too drunk to be careful. . . . He sprang suddenly, driving with a lifted knee and a stiff left. Lash sidestepped with the light feet of a dancer and jolted him hard in the belly. The blow landed with a thud. It knocked a grunt out of Gullion and stopped him in his tracks for a moment. Lash, seeing him weak, threw a long right at his nose and Gullion sat down with blood spilling down over his lips and chin while the crowd gave a yell for Lash.

He seemed to be having it all his own way and Gullion was getting what he had begged for. But they didn't know Gullion. Hard-headed and thick-skinned, made of bone and wire he was a fighter of the kind that gets drunk on his own blood. Knuckles had been broken on his skull without stopping him. He rose, spitting blood and snorting, and ran in again, took a right on his neck, ducked under a left and got a crushing under hold.

Lash bent in his arms like a sapling in a storm and they went down heavily together while the crowd yelled. As they fell Lash got a fast grip with his left hand in Gullion's thick woolly hair and with a right palm against his chin, twisted his opponent's head, bound to turn him over or break his neck. He was about to turn him, too, when his thumb slipped within reach of Gullion's mouth and yellow teeth closed on it. For a moment Lash writhed in agony, then drove his knee with a desperate jerk into Gullion's stomach, knocking the wind out of him and making him open his mouth. As the hold broke he got to his feet, knocking Gullion back with a short jab. Too mad now to be careful he followed him up, slugging with all his might. Gullion, cunning as a coon, saw his chance, sidestepped and tripped Lash with a leg between his feet. Lash fell forward and Gullion pounced on him just as he turned over, pinning his right arm with a great left hand and his body with both knees.

Now Gullion had what he wanted—a chance to gouge. Now unless Sam Lash yelled for mercy he stood a chance to lose an eye or the side of his face.

They all crowded round the struggling two with intent unsmiling faces. No one had any right to interfere. If Lash was beaten he could yell and then they would pull the two apart.

Gullion lifted his right hand with fingers spread and stiff, jabbed again and again at Lash's eyes and Lash fended him off with his left as best he could and writhed in an effort to bring a knee into play. Gullion scratched skin off his face and broke his lips. . . . Both of them were half blind with sweat and blood and breathing in hoarse gurgling gasps like animals shot through the lungs. . . .

2

When Lola ran into the circle of firelight they all stood staring at her pop-eyed. They had forgotten her existence.

With her long black hair hanging loose, stamping the ground and yelling shrill furious Spanish, she was almost as startling to them as an apparition of the dead.

"Quick, quick, quick!" she shrilled. "Stop them! Stop them! He's killing him. He's killing my blond one. . . . Stop them, you pigs!"

But nobody moved quick enough to suit her. She ran over to the fire, picked up a blazing stick of fat pine, made a dash at Gullion and began beating him furiously over the head and shoulders with short awkward strokes. Gullion ducked this way and that, then jumped up, slapping at his head and ears with both hands like a man fighting bees, knocking hot coals and ashes out of his hair. He barely glanced at the woman. A hot coal had slipped down inside his pants behind and he went writhing and squirming around almost tying himself in a knot to get it out. . . .

Sam Lash stood up slowly and with some trouble. Blowing, bloody, naked to the waist, scratched and dirty he stood looking at her with his mouth open and not a word to say. But she had enough for both of them.

"You fool!" she shrilled. "What do you mean by fighting with that dirty pig? If you had trouble with him why didn't you shoot him? That you should roll around in the dirt that way and let him try to scratch your eyes out! Do you think I want a blind fool for a husband?"

For a moment she stood looking at him, her breasts rocking, her black eyes brimming with rage. Then she went up to him, took him by the hand, spoke with scornful tenderness.

"Come with me," she said. "I will wash your cuts. . . ."

Docile and wordless the warrior was led away. The others looked after the pair a moment and then a shout of laughter broke from them all at once. . . .

3

When Sam came back to the fire some of the men were spreading blankets and others were lighting final pipes. Gullion came up from the creek where he had been washing blood and dirt off himself. He was singing happy. He spied Lash and came over to him and stuck out his hand and they shook.

"That was a good ruction we had while it lasted, boy," he said. "Ef that little chili o' yorn hadn't set me afire I'd of made you holler, shore as hell. . . ."

He went poking around among the packs, found a haunch of venison and held it up.

"Ho boys," he shouted. "Who's for meat? This chile feels like chawin'. I'll cut it an' cook it. . . . Ef we cain't fight we kin eat!"

CHAPTER TEN

I

ROM Taos north to the British territories there was one place where a man could sit down and feel sure his hair was safe—one place where he could leave horse, beaver, woman or money and hope to find it there when he got back. That place was Bent's Fort on the Arkansas. There anyone could eat, trade, and stop as long as he was of a mind to. Any trader or trapper could there get a stake on credit.

Bent's Fort had walls fifteen feet high and three feet thick made of adobe mixed with Navajo wool. On top of the walls, all the way around, grew cactus of the low thick fat-leaved kind bearing red and yellow flowers in the spring.

Nothing could climb over the walls of Bent's Fort, nothing could knock them down and they couldn't be set afire. Double oak gates at either end were sheathed in iron. Inside was a courtyard with stores and living rooms all around it and a fur-press in the middle. Over the front gate was a square tower room with windows on all four sides and a long telescope mounted on a swivel, and Bent kept one man there all the time to watch. The watchman could spot a dust-cloud twenty miles at least, for wide flatlands lay on both sides of the valley. The cottonwoods that grew low and thick along the muddy Arkansas were the only cover as far as eye could see.

Two round towers with little rifle windows sat on opposite corners. Inside, their walls were hung with sabers, buffalo lances, muskets and horse pistols. Dust was all over them for they had never been used. Every year Comanche, Rapaho, Ute, Pawnee, Cheyenne and sometimes Sioux came here to trade beaver and buffalo robe for liquor, paint, beads, scarlet cloth, knives, guns and sugar. Nearly always from the Fort you could see rows of tepees up and down the valley. Sometimes Indians full of liquor painted their faces black and danced the war dance within sight of the walls and sometimes Ute and Rapaho met there and fought out their ancient grudge with shrill yells and flights of arrows shot from under the necks of running ponies. Warriors of five tribes camped under the walls of Bent's Fort but none of them ever attacked it, partly because it was too strong and partly because William Bent, who married the Cheyenne Owl Woman, was honest to Indians.

Down by the river was an adobe ice house and Bent hired a hunter to keep it filled with meat. Travelling buffalo often crossed the Arkansas in sight of the Fort by thousands, antelope drank at the river every day and deer hid in the brushy bottoms. For change the hunter went to the mountains and brought back packmule loads of bighorn and elk.

Bent's wagons hauled furs to the Missouri and came back loaded with flour, sugar, coffee, dried fruit and bacon.

Bent's cook was a nigger named Green and he used pots big enough to drown a man in. When a meal was ready he tolled a bell that hung in the courtyard and all that could hear it were welcome to the table. Bent never knew how many he fed but sometimes there were hundreds. Women ate at a separate table, Indian children got fat hanging around the kitchen door and squaws filched from the storerooms. Bent made such enormous profits on his trade that he could feed them all and never know it.

At Bent's there were dances, weddings, horse races and games but few fights. Bent wouldn't have them. Who came there got his rights and held his peace. . . .

2

When Sam Lash came out to saddle and pack
the Fort was very quiet. Nearly all mountain men
were already on their way to high country for the
fall trapping season because some of them would
go as far south as Sonora and some as far north
as the Yellowstone. Utes and Rapahoes now were
camped in the mountains and Cheyenne were
planting corn far to the East. About the Fort
were only a few that worked for Bent, and
women and children the trappers had left behind
and all of these were indoors now because it was
hot. The only sound in the courtyard was the
singing of mockingbirds that Owl Woman kept
there in wooden cages. Bent's pair of tame eagles
roosted sleepy on the roof and the watchman in
his tower looked drowsily at the smoke of his
own pipe.

Sam Lash was the only man of his kind around
the place and he should have been on his way a
week before and knew it. He felt like a squaw-
man hanging around when everyone else had
gone.

His face was pale and there was trouble in his
eyes as he saddled his big roan in the high-walled
corral behind the Fort.

The roan was fat and even a little pot-bellied from idle days on good grass and his coat was smooth and shiny. He looked like a ripe strawberry. When Sam tightened the cinch with a knee against him he laid back his ears and swung his head, nipping at Sam's elbow half in play and half in anger.

Sam worked slowly at getting ready because he didn't like what came after. He tied his rucksack on behind the saddle and stood off and looked at his horse. The roan was a good horse and for the mountains a big horse, sixteen hands high, wide between the forelegs, short-coupled, with an arched neck and heavy mane and tail of mixed black and gray. He had a deep dark eye with no white showing—he was a horse you could trust. He had a fine spring in his haunches and could beat an Indian pony for a quarter mile, and yet he was a good trail horse with power enough to lift a heavy load over mountains. There was good blood in him but he was mustang enough to rustle a living wherever he found himself. He would eat cottonwood and scrub oak in a pinch and dig to grass through a foot of snow. He would stick around camp like a dog and come to Sam when he whistled.

Sam Lash rested his eyes on his horse and felt

better. He longed to be in the saddle and moving. He craved saddle leather as a hungry man craves food.

When he had finished with his horse he went and caught his packmule, which he called Buckskin because she was the color of new buckskin with a black stripe from neck to tail and a stripe across her withers. She was a Spanish mule, sired by a burro and dammed by a mustang mare and no taller than her dam, but she was built trim as a deer with little round hooves hard as flint. Sam had bought her off a Mexican mule train and she had to be handled Mexican style. First he blindfolded her with a beaded buckskin blinder that fitted over her ears. Then he put the grass pad on her back and cinched it up with a wide grass cinch that bit into her belly as though it would cut her in two. But that was only because she blew herself full of wind. At the same time she hunched her back, laid her ears and made her skin crawl and twitch all over, but she wouldn't move a foot with her blinder on. She went through the same show every time and it didn't mean anything. There wasn't a sore on her back. Sam slapped her on the rump and threw the *alforjas* across the pad. He piled his possibles into them, balancing the load with care, and threw on top his Navajo blanket and his squaw-tanned buffalo robe, folded square. Then he made it all fast with a rawhide rope tied in a squaw hitch and pulled the blinder off. Buckskin let out her wind in a deep sigh and hitched over on three legs and looked around at him as much as to say, Thank God that's over.

Sam started for the courtyard and then stopped and looked back at his animals standing there strong and ready, their sleek hides shining in the sun. . . . They had never looked so good to him.

3

When he went into the dim room where he had lived so much in ten days, he stopped a minute in the doorway to get his eyes used to the dim light.

Lola was lying face down on the *zaguan* with her bare arms up around her head and her long black hair spread over them. The odor and feel of her long thick hair had been upon him for ten days. He felt as though he were trapped and tangled in her long black hair.

The old woman Louisa sat on the floor over again the wall with her knees drawn up under her chin. She was so skinny she could fold herself up like a Barlow knife. Her black *reboso* was wrapped all around her and hooded over her head. Thin wisps of gray hair leaked out from

under it and fell across her face which was shrivelled like a potato in the sun. Her almost tooth-
less mouth was a slit under her great bony nose.
She sucked at a little flat cornhusk cigarette and
smoke leaked in a thin steady stream from her
nose as though she were afire and smouldering
inside. . . . She looked as though something inside were burning her out and she was slowly
shrivelling in the heat. Her little deepset eyes
were on Sam all the time unblinking and they
made him uncomfortable. . . . Whether she was
a witch or not she sure looked like the Devil.

All the Mexicans and some of the whites believed she turned into a cat or a coyote at night
and went around working spells. They claimed
that she had cat eyes in the morning and that was
why she kept them covered with her shawl. . . .
Whether she had or not she was a mean looking
old wench and Sam wished she was out of there.

She had hated him from the first. She had
never given him a smile. . . . Maybe she never
smiled anyway, at least not at a man. She hung
around the Fort and worked for any woman she
could. She was a nurse and a midwife and knew
all kinds of big medicine. She had fastened onto
Lola from the first and had taken good care of
her, no doubt of that. Lola would have had a
worse time without her. She had waited on Lola

hand and foot, washed and fed and dressed her.
. . . They said she had been a beauty once and
some fellow had rolled her and left her big and
she had cursed him and he had died. Ever since
then she had been a witch and a midwife and sold
charms that kept off bad luck and brought love.
If she spit in your eye you would die before morning, so the Mexicans believed.

Sam took no stock in such notions himself but
he was afraid of old Louisa. He would have liked
to send her out of the room but he knew she
wouldn't go.

What was Lola going to say to him now? They
had had it all out two or three times over a bucket
of tears but they would have it all out again. . . .
He had to go, there was no two ways about that.
. . . He had never known women could be so
hard to handle. . . .

But when she raised her head he knew she
wasn't going to put up another fight. Her eyes
were wide with the weariness of spent emotion
and her mouth was soft and bowed, craving pity.
. . . She came up to him and put her arms
around him and rested herself upon him, clinging
to him all over.

"Don't go, *querido*," she begged in her soft
Spanish. "I am nothing without you now. If you
go and don't come back I am lost. . . . I know

you mean to come back, but what if you die?
What if Indians kill you or a bear? . . . I
dreamed of you last night with blood on your
head. . . . Please, my *querido,* you cannot
go. . . ."

Her voice started to rise but it broke into
tears and she hung on him, pleading with her
arms and her breast and her soft mouth lifted
toward his, hardened against her. . . . There
was no fight left in her.

Sweat stood out on his face. He felt as though
his muscle and bone had turned to water.

He had given her everything he had for the
time being. She rested upon him now only as a
burden. But how she weakened and softened him!
How hard it was to break her so tender hold!
No grip of a strong man in a fight had ever been
so hard to break. . . . In nights together she
had torn him apart and taken him into her. He
rent his own flesh now when he pulled away. . . .
It had never been like this before. . . .

He had to go! He clung desperately to his
resolution. He was a mountain man, a trapper,
not a squaw-man. . . . Even if they went back
to Taos together, even if her family took him in,
he could not sit around like a greaser against a
wall. He would rot on a Mexican life of idleness. . . .

They had fought it all out before. There was no use fighting it out again. And anyway she was beaten. He lifted her and carried her back to the *zaguan,* laid her down, kissed her. . . .

"I have to go," he told her quietly. "I will come back—nothing will kill me. I will come back sooner than you think. . . ."

4

Her wail followed him out the door, stinging his ears. Worse than that, so did the old witch Louisa. He was aware of her following like a black moving shadow across the courtyard. He went into the corral and shut the gate and heard it open and close again behind him.

She squatted there against the wall in the bright sunlight with the hood of her shawl hiding her eyes. . . . When he turned upon her, uncertain what to say, she rose slowly and pointed a long skinny finger at him.

"*Maldito gringo!*" she shrilled. "A curse on your soul and body!

"A curse on your father and mother!

"May the devil fly away with your brothers and sisters and the cousin of your grandmother!

"May coyotes devour the bones of your uncles and aunts!"

She came toward him until her finger was shaking right under his nose.

"Son of a sleeping mother who was too tired to eat!" she yelled. "For this your soul will lodge in purgatory until it goes to hell! For this I will haunt you and follow you with bad luck while you live on earth! For this your gun will miss fire and your horse will stumble. Indians will dog your trail and storms will strike you!"

Sam climbed into his saddle and rode for the corral gate, bending low like a man running from thunder. When he pulled the gate closed behind him its bang cut her off in the middle of another flight.

Then she came out and stood in the gateway and her parting curse came to his ears, faint but furious with the ancient hatred of waiting woman for man who rides away. . . .

"Gringo pig! Misbegotten son of a drunken father who knew not what he did! Wherever you go I am with you and you are damned!"

CHAPTER ELEVEN

AM forded the river, swift yellow water gurgling almost belly deep around his horse's legs.

Water was still high from melting snow but dropping as white patches dwindled on purple mountains far to the west. . . .

That old woman she would give anybody the creeps. And what could you do? You couldn't shut her up. If he was a greaser now he would be scared. . . . He looked back over his shoulder half expecting to see a black thing gliding after him like a shadow over the ground, but he saw only the Fort asleep in the sun. . . . Lola would be all right there. . . .

That old wench believed she flew around at night all right. She had a story she told when anybody would give her a drink and a dollar about how she went out on the prairie north of Taos one night and all the sagebrush was hung with rubies and sapphires and under one bush was a prairie-dog hole that opened up big as a door and she went in and down, down, down until she came to a big lighted room where many tall men and women were having a *baile* and all of them were dressed in silk and satin and smiling. Among them walked a great goat on its hind legs and a snake that stood up six feet high on its tail and it had red eyes and a red forked tongue. It went up to every man and every woman and put its tongue in the mouth of each and it was the tongue of wisdom. It put its tongue into her mouth and fire ran through her body like lightning through a tree and everything went black and she was alone on the prairie, but the tongue of wisdom was in her mouth and ever since then she had known everything. . . . She believed it had happened all right. If you doubted her she would offer to take you out there and show you the bush and the prairie-dog hole, and if you laughed at her she would curse you in a way that would make anybody stand back. . . . She was loco. . . . All witches and medicine men were loco but strange things happened. . . .

An unseen terrible world crowded around him and he spurred into a trot. . . . He remembered a hound dog back in Kentucky that howled every time somebody was going to die and it was never known to fail and the black cat that crossed his grandmother's path before she took her death of ague and the devil that came up out of the Boiling Spring and wrastled with Black Harris, and Joe Meek paying a Crow medicine man two ponies to make medicine and tell him where his lost partner was and he went there and found his bones. . . .

He spurred up through low hills and came out on the mesa. Cool wind whipped at his face and rich purple-tinged country rolled away forty miles to blue mountains. A real world began to claim him. He lived again in his eyes. . . . Scattered antelope were pale dots all over the prairie. They ranged solitary now when does were dropping their fawns. He would pick off a yearling buck somewhere and take along haunch and saddle. . . . Tracks of five unshod ponies and a *travois* making two lines showed him where a Ute family had crossed the day before and a thin wisp of smoke miles off to the southeast told him they were camped at the forks of the Purgatoire and the Arkansas. They were on their way to the mountains and nothing to bother about.

Every mile he put between him and the Fort made woman and witch seem more remote and unreal to him. The country took him back to itself seizing him by every sense. Wind heavy with earth smell washed the memory of her hair out of his nose and the steady beat of hoof on sod soothed away the sting of curses.

[139]

When he saw an easy chance he dropped off his horse behind a rise in the land, crawled up on a feeding antelope and killed it. While he was skinning he noticed a coyote sitting on its haunches a hundred yards away waiting for him to finish. . . . Funny how when you killed one always showed up from nowhere. In winter when they were hungry they would follow for days and get tamer all the time, more and more like a dog. A lone lobo wolf would do it too but he stayed farther off. . . . Never a bobcat or a cougar. They ate only what they killed and stayed away from men. . . . As he rode away with fresh meat rolled in a hide on top of his pack he looked back and saw the coyote eating at his leavings. A little later he was surprised to see it loping along about a hundred yards to the right. It was staying with him. That was unusual at this time of year. It made him faintly uneasy. . . . It was a bitch coyote. He could see her low-hanging dugs. She had pups somewhere and wouldn't go far—unless she had lost them.

When he dropped into the valley of the Purgatoire late in the afternoon the coyote still was with him and when he stopped to camp she was sitting on her haunches with her tongue hanging out just a hundred yards away.

"I can't seem to get shet of bitches," he re-

marked out loud and laughed at himself a little
ruefully. He was tempted to shoot her but he
didn't.

With two hours of daylight still before him
he made camp leisurely. He turned his stock loose
without hobbling them because he knew they
wouldn't move far on such good grass. It was a
foot high in the bottoms. Down along the sandy
edge of the river he gathered water-borne wood
that would burn hot and quick and make a fine
bed of coals.

He loved a camp like this with good grass and
plenty wood. To spread his robe and blanket
he picked a high bare spot back against the sandhills that bounded the narrow valley. Then he
built his fire and broiled the antelope's liver. The
other meat was still too fresh. He was very par-
ticular about meat and knew all ways to cut and
cook and cure it but other victuals didn't mean
much to him. He had a round loaf of bread they
had given him at the Fort. It was made of white
flour hauled all the way from the Missouri. He
broke it in half and munched it with his meat but
it tasted flat to him.

When he had finished eating he went down to
the stream, lay flat and took a long deep drink.
He lifted a dripping face to watch a beaver swimming across the stream. The beaver saw the

movement, slapped the water with a flat tail and dived—swatchoog! Way down the river he heard another answering swatchoog. When one slapped and dived every beaver in the water caught the signal and did the same. Beaver couldn't talk but they kept touch with each other better than men. A lone beaver would do nothing but travel along the bank and make mudpies and squirt his medicine into them until he found where a mate had left a message for him. You couldn't keep them apart and they stuck together till one was dead. . . .

He sat back against a tree and kept quiet and pretty soon he could see three or four beaver swimming around. This stream had been trapped for years but it was hard to get the last of them in a place like this. It was bad trapping because the beaver built no dams or lodges. They lived in holes under the bank. You had to wade in deep water and the bottom was all quicksand and wouldn't hold a stake or a slide pole. . . . Little mountain streams where they built long dams were the soft picking. He remembered a place he and Gullion found way up near timberline in the San Juan mountains where the beaver had dammed a stream a foot wide again and again all down a canyon so it looked like great silver stair-steps set in dark spruce and yellow aspen that

[142]

mirrored in the water. That was a pretty place and a regular goldmine. All they had to do was cut the dams and set traps in the breaks with slide poles. Beaver would come to mend the breaks and get caught and drown and more would come and use the dead beaver to mend the break. They took two hundred pounds of fur out of that canyon and many of the peltries were almost black and worth eight dollars a pound. They worked from dawn till dark like corncrackers in harvest time for two weeks and lived on the fat rich meat of beavertail till they couldn't bear the sight of it. He would give something pretty for a stewed beavertail right now but it was against his morals to kill a beaver in June unless it was the only meat in sight.

It was dusk now of a clear still evening and everything was astir. Over his head bullbats dipped and zoomed in mating play. Pale gray jack-rabbits came out in a little open place on the bank and played silent as ghosts, stopping to cock long ears and lift muzzles to the wind, fading into the brush when a coyote yapped. Crickets and frogs began their music and somewhere in a bush a little bird sang, waited and sang again. . . . He stretched his legs and drew a deep breath. Alone and miles from men, for the first time in weeks he sat safe and easy.

When it got dark he went back to camp and piled big chunks of cottonwood on his fire so it flamed high. Out of a beaded buckskin bag that hung around his neck he took a red sandstone pipe and fitted a long reed stem into it. He filled it with a mixture of bright yellow Virginia tobacco and red *kinnik-kinnik,* made from the inner bark of willow. With a coal from the fire he lit up and smoked in long slow thoughtful puffs. Like an Indian he treated tobacco with reverence. He smoked only at night and then he gave himself wholly to his smoking.

The roan and the buckskin, with their bellies round from good grass and deep drinks, came and stood just outside the circle of firelight which shone into their great warm contented eyes. They always came close to camp that way when they were on good grass and he gave them sugar or Indian corn when he could to keep them in the habit. The roan would come to a whistle and that was worth a lot to him. In fact a man couldn't travel alone without a horse he could trust. One that wandered far from camp would soon belong to an Indian and one that was hard to catch when you needed him would cost you your hair some time. . . . The buckskin mule was contrary but she stayed with the roan and like most Mexican mules she could smell Indian a long way off and always gave a snort of warning. If the buckskin snorted in the night there was either Indian or panther in the brush.

He felt good there in the small red circle of firelight with all his things around him. Everything he needed lay within reach of his hand. Horse and rifle, pack and saddle, trap and blanket—with these he was complete and independent as a wild animal. Once more he was whole and alone. . . . He who had been caught and torn apart once more felt whole and free. . . .

As he always did last thing at night he made a circle all around his camp, looked and listened, noticed the wild things were unfrightened at their play and that the sky was clear. . . . The only thing he could see that bothered him at all was the eyes of a coyote shining yellow in the dark just beyond the range of his fire. . . .

CHAPTER TWELVE

I

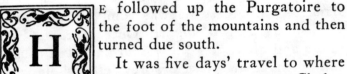E followed up the Purgatoire to the foot of the mountains and then turned due south.

It was five days' travel to where he was supposed to meet Chabonard and the others and the going was good. Water, wood, and game waited for him at every stop and summer storms held off to give him bright clear days.

It was good going but every mile of it seemed harder for him. Day by day his temper got worse so that he cursed his animals for no reason at all. He seemed to forget how to do things. Once he crawled up on a drinking buck to kill it and forgot to shake powder into the pan of his rifle so that when he pulled the trigger it only clicked. The buck went bouncing up the mountain, stopping once to look back at him and was gone before he could try again. He had never done such a thing before.

Whenever he saw a coyote—and there was one

in sight most of the time—he felt like shooting it, but he never did.

Each day he was in a worse temper than the day before.

His days were bad but it was the nights he couldn't stand. He never had another peaceful night like that first one when it felt so good to be alone and on the trail again.

He thought he would forget her until it was time to go back. He thought he could leave her behind as he had left other women. Instead he found she was still with him just as she had been that night in Taos after the *baile*.

She came back to him first at night when he was asleep and then in the daytime too. . . . If he was not bewitched he might as well have been. . . .

While he rode along trying to keep his mind on trail and weather, on track and sign, as a man must if he goes alone and keeps his hair, she came back to him in every different moment he had known her. He cursed her because she made him lose his way and forget whether he had crossed the north fork of Turkey Creek or not. When he should have been watching for a big boulder where you turn left and go over the ridge, he was remembering how she came forward to meet him when he did his breakdown at the *baile* in Taos.

. . . Neither of them knew what they were getting into then. It was like when two fellows start to spar in play and first thing you know one draws blood and they have got to fight it out. . . . When she pressed herself against him that was what started all the trouble. Before that he was half scared of her because she was so different from what he was used to. He couldn't get past the fact that she was a *rico*. But after that she was woman to him and her clothes and her family didn't matter. He felt then as though if he could get to her they could take him out and shoot him afterwards if they wanted to. He was just like a rutty buck with a swollen neck that won't stop for man, panther or devil when he gets on the trail of a doe. . . . He would have climbed through her window that night if it hadn't been barred, and she would have helped him too, with old Baulin down on his knees sawing out music by the yard.

When she horned into his fight with Gullion that made him feel queer. . . . He never thought she would have had the guts. . . . That set him back about fifteen years and made him feel like a kid being led home by his Mama. They all gave him the horse laugh but he didn't give a damn.

She shone that night but she was plenty scared afterwards. When they stood up to be married in

the Fort she was shaking like a cold dog and it
made him feel sorrowful. He was glad when old
Louisa took her and led her away and made a
fuss over her. She was used to that and it made
her feel better. . . . When it came to going to
her he had the fantods himself. After all he had
done to get her he felt short and scared and he
had never felt that way about a woman before.
. . . When he went to the door of the room
where she was he could hardly move a hand to
open it and when he finally did she was standing
there with a scared mouth and eyes as big as dollars and a serape she had grabbed up wrapped
around her. One big tallow candle made unsteady
light in a draft. . . .

He stood there in the door and for a minute
he couldn't say a word or lift a foot. . . . Her
naked arms and shoulders and the dip of her
breast were so much prettier than he had known
anything could be. . . . He couldn't believe she
was a real woman waiting there for him. She
seemed more like a dream woman same as she
was now. . . . When she saw how she had flab-
bergasted him that seemed to make her feel better. Fear died slowly out of her eyes and she began to smile, a sort of come-and-get-me smile, and
then she let her serape slip little by little, and
then she dropped it and blew the candle out. . . .

He spurred his horse so it jumped and snorted and went thundering down the trail. . . . He ran from a wraith of memory as he had never run from living foe. . . . He wasn't going back—that was one thing sure!

He pulled the roan up short, realizing that he was a fool to go slamming along that way in a country where he knew Indians were travelling. She would be the death of him if he didn't get her out of his head. . . .

Scared by his own recklessness he went slowly the rest of the day and kept a sharp lookout for track and sign. Late in the afternoon he picked up two unshod tracks, made by a horse ridden and one led. He followed cautiously till the tracks turned west and apparently went over the range. That made him feel better. Pony tracks like that meant probably a Cheyenne or Comanche warrior on a lone warpath and that was the worst kind of Indian to have around. An Indian with no squaw along was twice as reckless and had about twice as much fight in him as one that dragged a family. . . . Come to think of it you could say the same of a white man.

As he rode along in the daytime she bothered him that way, once in a while. The memory of her seemed to stick to his skin as though she had put her brand on him and the burn still hurt. But he was schooled to keep his eye peeled all the time and one thing and another called him back to where he was. . . . At night it was different. She had him at her mercy then. Each night she was with him a little more than the night before. Asleep he dreamed about her and lying awake he remembered the feel of her arms and threw out his own to clutch a ghost. . . . One night he couldn't stand it, got up and went down the creek and plunged desperately into a deep pool. The water ran straight from snow banks on the peaks and he came out dripping and chilled, rid of her for a minute. He dried himself with his shirt and then stood there feeling safe and untroubled again.

"I went away too soon, that's all," he decided.

But he thought he saw eyes of a cat or a coyote shining in the dark and that made him remember the old woman's curses. He crawled back into his blankets and hid his head.

One night he waked up sure he had heard her wail the way she did when they quarrelled before he left. That always made him feel helpless. Just when he was making it clear that he had to go, that there was nothing on earth for him to do but go back to the mountains, she would bury her face in her hands and let a long caterwaul. . . . All Mexican women were great on that hollering.

When somebody died they howled all night. . . .
Whenever she wailed that way he felt as though
he was killing her although he had never lifted a
hand against her much as he had felt like it a
time or two when she was so contrary and
wouldn't listen to reason. He felt even now sometimes as though he would like to go back and beat
her for pestering him this way when he had to go
about his business.

He waked up with the echo of her voice in his
ears. He was sure he had heard something. He
sat up and listened and after a little while he
heard it again and he knew what it was—a mountain lion on the prowl. They made a noise just
like a woman only it sounded kind of crazy like
a woman out of her mind. The damned thing
would scream every few minutes and it made him
uneasy as a cow in a thunderstorm. He would lie
down to sleep and just about the time he was
somewhere near it he would hear that screech
again. . . . A man named Dawson he trapped
with in the Yellowstone never believed a lion
screeched at all. He believed the noise was made
by the spirit of a woman that had died. . . . It
was a fact you couldn't find anyone that had ever
seen a lion screech. But you seldom saw one anyway unless dogs put it up a tree. They were the
sneakiest critters in the mountains. Sometimes one

would follow a man for days and nights and he would find tracks and maybe hear a screech but never see hair nor hide of it. A lion never ate the leavings of a kill and never jumped a man neither. It just trailed along and watched. . . . The damn thing screeched off and on all night and he never did sleep good. . . . Lola was all right there at the Fort. It was the safest place in the mountains. She was just as safe there as she would have been in Taos. . . .

Next morning he went out and looked for tracks and found them, big around as the crown of a hat, where the lion had drunk at the creek. It was a big one.

Staring at the tracks he could picture the deadly bow-curve of the crouching back, the muscular upthrust of the withers, the yellow-eyed angular head that lapped and listened and lapped again. . . . At least he knew it was a lion. . . . Of course he knew that anyway. . . . But there was something uncanny about those big sneaky critters that were nearly always just a shadow and a voice. . . . All day long he had a followed feeling and he even looked over his shoulder a time or two. He didn't see anything but he heard one again that night and every time it yelled he waked up with a start. . . .

Loss of sleep began to tell on him. He felt

skittish like a man that's just getting over a spree and he found it harder than ever to keep his mind on his business. While he rode one way his mind kept going back the other. . . . She was never all there at once. . . . Her small hand would grab him or her hair would blow in his face, he would taste her mouth or feel the moist cling of her hot arms and it was more real than when it happened. . . . Never before had anything come back over him that way. . . . Could that old woman have fed him something in his soup? She sold a kind of medicine to Mexican girls that was supposed to make their *queridos* love them more—something that was bound to bring a man back. . . .

He spurred the roan and slapped the mule on the rump. Buckskin, insulted, jumped out of the trail, squatted and whirled quick as a rabbit and ran back the way she had come. Red and cursing fit to curl a gun barrel he put out after her and headed her back toward the south.

"You travel where yo're pointed, you contrary little bitch!" he shouted. "This outfit's bound for the Gila!"

2

Noon of the fifth day he topped a ridge and looked down on the valley of the Cimarron.

[154]

It lay just where the mountains met the prairie on the well watered eastern slope.

The Cimarron Creek came down from high ridges, bare of timber and topped with naked rock, through a deep box canyon that widened here into a pretty meadow half a mile long with the creek in the middle showing white riffles and silver pools through willow cover.

It was a favorite stopping place for red men and white. Water, wood and grass were as good here as ever you would find. It was sheltered from the storms and horses could forage in the meadow all winter long. . . . No place could a man kill more kinds of meat. The best of the buffalo country rolled away to the east, purple-tinged as always after spring rains, patched with dark moving cloud shadows. Way down there he could see scattered herds and right in the mouth of the canyon antelope were dotted thick as sheep in a pasture. Black-tail deer abounded in the heavy cover of the ridges, cow elk drank at the creek every morning and the old bulls were near timber-line growing new antlers. Far up toward melting snow ranged the big horned mountain sheep from which the country took its Mexican name.

It was a sweet place and a dangerous one, for all kinds of Indians passed here—Apaches and

Utes coming down from the mountains to hunt buffalo, Cheyenne and Comanche coming up from the prairies to raid the Mexican settlements across the range. Much blood had wet the meadows of the Cimarron.

Here he was supposed to meet his party—unless they had gone on and left a message marked on the ground for him to follow.

With weary legs he climbed a rocky spur of the ridge and studied the little valley. He knew where they would have camped and even if their camp had been out of sight he would have seen horses in the meadow. . . . There was not a horse or a man in sight.

When he knew they had gone on it seemed to him the last of his energy oozed out of his legs. He sat down limp and discouraged. . . . Fighting against a backpull he couldn't understand he had come this far and he had counted on his fellows to carry him along. . . .

Riding with the bunch would have been different. Singing and chanting they rode and he would have been swept along with them. He couldn't have gone back then. . . . Why had he started so late?

Chanting to the drum of hooves they were riding over the range and down the valley, west through the Navajo country and south to the

Gila. . . . It was the same route he had followed
on his first trip. . . . That was a trip to remember—the trip when first he lifted hair and trapped
beaver and proved himself a mountain man. . . .
That trip in his mind now had the strangeness
of a remembered dream. He had felt then as
though he could go on forever. There had been
nothing anywhere that called him back. No place
on earth meant more to him than last night's
camp. . . . It was different now.

His animals were gaunt and he was tired. He
would have to stop a day at least and kill meat
and rest and let his stock graze. Then he would
have to go alone day after day on their trail. He
had gone alone as much as any man in the mountains but it seemed like he couldn't go another
mile alone now. Never before had the mountains
seemed so empty to him. Never before had he
held back from a trail. . . .

He rode down into the valley and got off his
horse. While the roan and the buckskin eagerly
munched new sprung bluegrass and wild oats, he
lay down by the creek and drank deep from a
pool where long shadowy forms of trout fanned
water clear as air with lazy tails.

He moved himself wearily to the shade of a
lone blue spruce that spread itself wide beside
the creek, leaned back against the trunk of it

with legs stretched heavy on the ground. It was still and bright and the little valley, rainwet and sunwarm, breathed a sweet heavy smell and a soft sleepy sound of locust, bee and water.

He felt as though something had shot him so far and there he lay aimless and spent. . . . It was so peaceful there it seemed as if he was not in the mountains but in a meadow on a farm back in Kentucky. That smell of grass and hum of bugs was like Kentucky. He could almost expect to hear the voice of a woman singing at her work somewhere in a hidden house. He wished someone would ring a dinner bell and all he had to do was get up and walk to it. He wished he didn't have to kill to eat.

The little valley would have made a farm. It had never struck him before. Here were timber and stone to build and land that would show black and rich under plow and water that would turn a mill and grass for a thousand cows. . . .

As always when a man sits still in the mountains life began to show and stir around him. Down the creek a hundred yards a doe came out of the brush and stood with little sharp feet close-planted and lifted head, studying the wind with a wet muzzle before she crossed the open. He knew she had been down to drink and had a fawn hidden in the timber and was eager to get back to it with heavy udders.

On a rock in the creek two water wrens appeared and bobbed and bowed to each other and flew away again.

Then came a pair of jays, flitting from bush to bush and shouting for everything to hear that they saw something strange.

They came and perched almost over his nose. They were deep indigo blue with black topknots and long tails tipped with black. They looked at him with bright inquisitive eyes, cocking their heads. He never moved a muscle and they decided he was some strange kind of a root growing out of that tree. They forgot him and began to chase each other roundabout in mating play.

Fluttering and screaming with excitement they flashed among green leaves, bright blue fragments of life for which the rest of the world had ceased to be.

Sam watched them with a fellow feeling so keen it hurt. He followed every move of the pirouetting eager cock bird and yearned with him for the moment of his triumph. It seemed as though nothing else mattered. His whole being hung upon a fluttering eagerness of poised desire.

Beautifully they coupled bodies bending up and down to meet in a quivering moment of ecstasy.

Screaming they flew away and the world was empty.

For a moment Sam Lash lay heavy-legged, inert. Then energy flowed into him as though it had come up from the earth—as though he had been a sprout of desire on the brown body of the urgent earth.

He jumped to his feet. He jumped the creek. He snatched the roan's astonished head out of the grass and gave the mule a kick.

"Out of that, you goddam burros!" he shouted, "This outfit's going back!"

CHAPTER THIRTEEN

I

LACK WOLF, southern Cheyenne, painted his face for battle and rode away alone.

He was twenty-one years old and this was the first time he had gone alone on a warpath. Unless he could return driving horses enough to please the father of Ameertschee he would never return at all. This he had vowed to the Maiyun. He was riding toward power and love or else he was bound for the camps of the dead and so his mood was solemn and exalted.

Leaving the white circle of lodges on the Arkansas, where his people had planted corn and squash and settled down for the summer, he rode for ten days across vast levels with blue mountains for his goal. He was safe on the prairie and he rode at a jog, the feet of his horse sinking to the fetlocks in spring growth of grass and primrose, singing the wolf songs which are always sung by lone warriors. Wolf songs are al-

ways about women for every lone warrior rides
away from a woman.

"Beloved," he sang sadly. "Why do you hide
from me in your lodge?"

"Beloved," he sang eagerly. "Come out of your
lodge that I may see you!"

"O beloved, I see you!" he sang and his voice
rolled across the prairie in a deep chant of triumph, making the antelope lift their heads and
jump, filling the air with the frightened wings of
crane and plover.

When he had finished his song he would ride
silent and sad for a while, knowing that he had
sung a dream, and then he would begin it all
over again.

Ameertschee he had loved as a child and had
waited for the day when her father shouted
proudly from the door of his lodge that she had
begun to be a woman. He had been the first to
wait outside her lodge to court her. Wrapped in
a red blanket so that only one eye showed he stood
patiently until she came out, fresh from the hands
of the old women who initiated her, smelling still
of the sacred smoke of white sage and juniper.
He opened his blanket in a wide gesture of invita-
tion. She swayed, she turned with her eyes on the
ground and backed into his arms so that she
might not know what she was doing. Wrapped in

a single blanket they stood for hours evening after evening.

Other men came to her lodge door for she had such small hands and ankles and such a deep ringing laugh and her father was rich. Dressed in blue buckskin trimmed with red porcupine quills and a sash of scarlet trade cloth about her waist, with the thick braids of her black hair hanging below her hips she turned the heads of young men as though with a strong hand. Sometimes in the evening five of them waited in a row to court her and she went in turn to the arms of each as was the custom. She went last to the arms of Black Wolf who stood next to the lodge door and in his arms she stayed long after all the others had gone. She let Black Wolf tear a wristlet from her arm and carry it away.

The parents of Black Wolf were poor and they died of the cholera. He was brought up in the lodge of some friends and they had not given him much. He had only two horses and one of those was not much good. He went on three war parties and each time he came back empty-handed. It became more and more clear that the Maiyun were not kind to him. He was a powerful youth and used a four-foot horn bow that few men could draw. He could shoot far and straight. None could ride better and he had a gift of managing bad horses. . . . He was a man of ability but the gods were against him.

Rich young men courted Ameertschee and sent friends to her father with offers of many horses. Black Wolf had no horses to offer. To buy a girl friends would give him a few, but as Ameertschee grew more and more popular it became clear to Black Wolf that he could not hope to have her unless his fortunes changed. He learned by gossip that when his name was mentioned in the lodge of her father they laughed. . . .

A Cheyenne girl would seldom marry against the wish of her parents. If she did run away with a man she loved, then he was expected to give her father even more horses than he would have sent as a bid for her hand.

Girls had been known to hang themselves when their fathers refused to let them marry the men they loved. But Ameertschee gave no sign that she longed for death because her parents laughed at Black Wolf. When she came home at dusk from digging roots on the prairie and found a long row of strong young men waiting to seize her in their arms her laugh rang out like the song of a lark.

Thunders-in-the-night was a dandy and his father was rich. Thunders-in-the-night spent much time plucking the whiskers out of his face with a bone tweezer, greasing his heavy black hair and painting his cheeks with striking designs in black and vermilion. Wearing beaded moccasins and new fringed leggins, wrapped in a clean red blanket, mounted on a white pony which he washed at the river every day, he would ride about the camp that women might admire his beauty. He had never counted a coup and all of his horses had been given him by his father and mother but he sat proud as a war chief and sang songs about what he was going to do.

At dusk Thunders-in-the-night waited outside her lodge for Ameertschee and step by step he moved to the chosen place next the lodge door.

When a messenger came to Black Wolf from the girl and demanded the wristlet he had torn off her arm, an invisible hand struck him a blow in the stomach. For an instant he saw his spirit standing apart from his body and he knew it longed to be off for the camps of the dead.

Black Wolf knew now that he must suffer and gain power and the help of the Maiyun or else he must die.

He did not go again to the lodge where Ameertschee lived. Instead he went to an old man named Standing Horse who had been a friend of his father and had made many sacrifices to gain power. He offered Standing Horse a pipe

and told him what had happened and what he
wanted to do. Standing Horse smoked gravely
for a long time and then he told Black Wolf to
come before sunrise the next morning.

When Black Wolf came the old man told him
to kneel and bend his back. With his fingers the old
man puckered the skin of the back in two places.
With a flint knife he cut through each pucker and
thrust a short stick of willow through the hole
just as one skewers meat on a stick for broiling
over the coals. Hot blood ran down the young
man's back and the pain was sweet to his soul.

Standing Horse then brought a rope about six
feet long. One end he tied through the nose of
a buffalo skull. At the other end were two thongs
of buckskin and these were looped over the little
sticks pinned through the flesh of the young man's
back.

When Standing Horse had prayed over him
Black Wolf set out to drag the buffalo skull four
times around the circle of the camp. As he walked
he prayed and sang. Now and then he jerked
hard upon the rope so that the skin of his back
was torn more and more and blood ran warmly
down his legs and into his moccasins. The skin
would tear but it would never break.

People looked at him as he passed with grave
and reverent looks and some of them made

prayers for him. When he passed the lodge where Ameertschee lived he sang more loudly. He hoped she saw his blood run. He hoped she saw his torn back and felt his pains. But he dared not turn his head to see if she was looking.

Toward the end of the day as he grew faint from thirst and loss of blood and sun beating upon his head visions began coming to Black Wolf in vague profusion. Once plodding with closed eyes he heard the drumming of many hooves in his ears and it seemed to him that he was riding swiftly among many horses and he took this for a good omen. But when he opened his eyes again he could see nothing. Lodges, trees and hills swam and vanished and he seemed alone on a great waterless plain and he heard far-away voices chanting and thought he must be near the camps of the dead. He staggered on across the aching plain, fell and got up again and fell once more. When next he saw the light he was in the old man's lodge and Standing Horse was bending over him, cutting little squares of skin off his back to set him free from his burden. Standing Horse buried these bits of flesh and made a prayer over them. Then he washed Black Wolf's lacerated back and gave him meat and water.

Black Wolf did not know whether he had won power or not. He had seen no clear vision of his destiny. Therefore next morning he went up in the hills to fast four days, taking with him nothing but a pipe and tobacco. He chose a crest of the sandhills that edge the valley and lay down on his belly facing east in the full glare of the sun. Three times a day he smoked a pipe, first pointing the stem up and down and to the four cardinal points, for the powers that rule the lives of men are above him and below him and in all directions. Every evening Standing Horse came and gave him a drink of water but he took no food.

After the second night visions bright and terrible began coming to Black Wolf so that he scarcely knew whether he was awake or asleep. He dreamed of the hunt and of killing buffalo, of drinking hot blood and plunging his hands into the steaming entrails of freshly killed game. The laughter of Ameertschee rang through his dreams, tantalizing him, for sometimes it seemed a taunt and sometimes a welcome. She appeared to him again and again. Once she walked toward him naked and great joy flooded him. Her long hair was unbound and the protective girdle of hair rope which is worn by all unmarried girls hung loose about her loins. He rose with a joyful shout of greeting and went to meet her. Then he saw that her head was turned backward and the shadow of a man fell beside her. . . . Black

Wolf awoke and lay alone on his hilltop. He was cold and the sky bent over him and looked at him with a million hard little eyes. He turned over and buried his face in the grass.

Most of his dreams were confusing. He saw himself in battle with Pawnees and Crows and even with white men who carried guns. He knew the swift hot ecstasy of a charge and felt sure that he was near to victory. And then he saw himself with his head covered with blood and it seemed to him that he was doomed to die in battle.

At last came a vision of himself riding swiftly through the night with many horses. He could not see how many but he heard the drum of hooves and dust was in his eyes and mouth and a wind-blown mane whipped his face. The horse under him was a great powerful beast and his flight was swift and smooth as that of a hawk. Nothing could overtake him and he rode until a white dawn showed behind him and he turned and sang to the rising sun in joy.

On the fourth morning Black Wolf sat up with difficulty. His ribs bulged like those of a lost horse in winter and his skin was covered with dirt and the bites of insects and scratched by rocks and burrs. The hills across the river wavered in his sight like ripples on water and the groves of cottonwood trees in the valley were black

[169]

masses that swam in a haze and shrank and swelled before his aching eyes. But Black Wolf was happy for he felt that he knew what he must do. He must ride west until he found a camp of enemies, then he must steal horses and ride east again. If he fought he would die but he must not fight. He must run like a leaf before the wind.

This plan which the gods had sent him was highly acceptable to Black Wolf for he had great skill in stealing horses and he knew that he stood little chance of victory in battle by himself. His enemies would likely be more than one and they might have guns among them. But let him once get his leg across a good horse and he would be hard to catch as a lizard.

Black Wolf knew that death in battle is a boon and that in the camps of the dead is neither toil nor sorrow but he preferred to stay on earth as long as he had a chance to get Ameertschee.

On the last morning of his fast, as he lay weak, he closed his eyes and saw himself riding into camp on a great horse and driving many other horses before him. He shouted in triumph and people poured from the lodges to welcome him. . . .

He opened his eyes and saw a magpie sitting on a limb of a juniper bush ten feet away. It was a magnificent bird, glossy greenish black with a

snow white belly and a white triangle on either
wing and its tail was a foot long. Turning its
head slowly from side to side it looked at him
first with one eye and then with the other. Black
Wolf watched it, scarcely breathing, for the magpie is a sacred bird and if he had won the pro-
tection of a special power it might well come
to him in the form of this bird.

As he looked the magpie seemed to swell until
it was large as an eagle and he heard a voice
which seemed to come from the bird saying "Follow me." Then the magpie shrank back to its
natural size and flew away straight into the West
until it was lost to sight.

2

Black Wolf rode his small spotted pony which
had no speed. He rode in a saddle of buffalo hide
stretched over a frame made of two forked willow sticks. Its willow stirrups were covered with
rawhide. On his left arm he wore a round shield
of buffalo hide which he had borrowed from old
Standing Horse, for young men do not own
shields. This shield was hung with eagle feathers
and it had the magic power of turning bullets.
In his right hand he carried a lance eight feet
long with a tip made from a butcher knife his

father had taken off the body of a white man killed in battle. Over his shoulder in a case of glossy otterskin, hung with tails, he carried his four foot bow and twenty new arrows. With his rawhide lariat he led a tall rawboned sorrel mare. She carried nothing but a buffalo-hide pad stuffed with grass and a pack containing a few pounds of pemmican and some extra moccasins. For this was his running horse, to be reserved for battle and hunting. She was an excellent buffalo horse and fast for a short run but her wind was none too good. Black Wolf longed above all for a horse that was faster than anything else on four legs and sound of wind and knee. However strong and brave a man may be he is no better than the horse he rides.

When he struck the Cimarron near the foot of the mountains he rode slowly and sang no more but watched on all sides and studied the ground for he was now in a country where he might meet anything. Mexican, gringo, Ute, Apache, Pawnee and Rapaho passed and camped here every summer.

Black Wolf camped in the edge of the timber, keeping both himself and his horses hidden. At dusk when smoke does not show far he made a fire no bigger than his two hands under a bower of brush and cooked meat on the coals, putting out the flame as soon as it was done. When dark came he picketed his horses on good grass, wrapped himself in his one blanket and lay down. He would not sleep until after midnight when his horses would be full and he could hide them among the trees. Meantime he lay looking at the stars gravely and thinking.

His body lay there but his spirit went back to the camp of his tribe for he belonged to it as a bee belongs to its hive and it was always in his mind.

He saw it as it would look in the morning when the lodges stand in a white circle beside the shining river. He saw the women going to fill their water jars and men and boys running in naked shouting groups to bathe while smoke of morning fires hung in blue wisps before the sun and yellow dust clouds on the hilltops showed where boys were driving down the horses.

While he lay there still and lonely he pictured all the happy stir of a beginning day when men rode away on their best horses to hunt and women set out to gather firewood and groups of young girls, laughing and playing tricks, climbed the hills with their long staves for digging roots. Children were scattered along the river, paddling in shallow water, making animal figures out of mud, playing games and practicing with tiny bows

[173]

and arrows as he had done such a few years ago.

For a while the camp would belong to women and to old men who sat in the shade smoking and telling tales of battles long ago and of gods and monsters, but late in the afternoon it was alive again as men came riding home on blood-stained horses and girls shouted a challenge from the hilltops. . . . He was among the young men who galloped out to meet them and fight a sham battle for their spoil of roots and berries and again he heard the ringing laughter of Ameertschee and again he caught her hand in play. . . .

Darkness fell upon the camp but it was not the awful empty darkness of night to a man alone. Fires now were akindle and those inside the lodges made them glow like moons spotted with moving shadows.

Now he was among the young men who stood outside the lodge doors waiting to court the girls while shouted invitations to feasts and storytellings went round the circle and children ran to summon those who might not hear. Above the murmur of many voices rose the music of flutes, of dance songs and gambling songs, and the droning chant of a medicine man. By this time all were gathered in warm groups inside the lodges, some to dance and sing and some to sit in polite circles and hear the words of famous storytellers. In some lodges men pledged themselves to the truth and told tales of war and hunting and challenged each other to tell better ones. In some lodges funny stories were told to shouts of mirth and in some the unchanging words of sacred legend fell upon a reverent hush—gods became visible, monsters lifted awful heads from lakes and rivers, beasts and birds spoke human words. . . . Slowly fires and voices died and the camp became quiet save for a few low tones from unseen couples and the weird notes of a flute from the hills where some lovesick boy roamed and played as they sometimes did all night. . . .

All night Black Wolf had roamed in the hills with his flute in the days when Ameertschee loved him. He walked in the dark and sat alone on hilltops thinking sometimes only of Ameertschee and sometimes only of the music he made. He heard ghosts run and whisper and spirit voices call. Wolves and wild cats came near and looked at him with eyes of green and yellow fire. Once Ameertschee heard him and came out of her lodge and called to him with the voice of an owl. . . .

Far from his people and alone for the first time in his life, Black Wolf loved them as he never had loved before. They had the magic quality of people in a story and the days of his happiness among them seemed hardly real. He wondered if ever he would sit safe in his lodge, the father of many children, the owner of many horses, telling tales of his prowess. . . . The wind spirit moaned in the forest and sleep came to Black Wolf sadly, like a prophecy of death.

3

As soon as daylight crept over the peaks he was up and alert, for the sun chases away ghosts and visions. He scouted the valley from end to end, up one side and down the other, finding old tracks of two small war parties of Utes, the deserted camp of a large band of trappers—and then the fresh trail of a large horse and a small mule, both shod.

The tracks puzzled him for they came down into the valley and then turned and went back the same way with the long strides that show hurry. No camp had been made. He found only where a man had lain by the creek to drink and where he had rested in the shade of a tree and where the butt of his rifle had touched the ground.

The white man with a rifle had ridden into the valley and then turned and ridden out in a hurry as though someone had chased him. Black Wolf

sought long and patiently for the tracks of what
had chased the white man out of the valley but
there was no mark. Of that he made sure, for
nothing could move on feet without leaving a
trace that he could see. This man must have been
chased by a ghost.

The trail was easy to follow and Black Wolf
followed it at a fast trot. He knew the canyon
where the man would almost surely camp but he
dismounted and crept up to every hilltop before
he rode over. He was going to make no mistakes.
The Maiyun had sent this white man for a gift to
him. With a white man's buffalo horse between
his knees, the ponies of the Utes and Crows
would be his easy gain. . . . Driving many
ponies, riding a tall shod horse he would return.
. . . And this man was careless. He rode hard
and without stopping to watch his back track.

Late in the afternoon Black Wolf saw a blue
ribbon of smoke rising from the small canyon
where he had known it would be.

Leaving the trail he rode far up in the timber
and hid his horses in an aspen thicket and stripped
himself to moccasins and breech clout, taking only
his bow and quiver and a knife in his belt. He
crept down the ridge as softly as a hunting bobcat. From a scrub oak thicket he peered down

upon a little glade where a spring filled a rock
basin with its slow drip and tall yellow pines en-
closed a few acres of good grass.

The white man had made his camp in the middle of the open as white men do, trusting to the
long range of his rifle for safety. His pack lay
on the ground and his animals were picketed near
it. The man was nowhere to be seen but Black
Wolf knew that he was probably back in the timber gathering more wood for his night fire.

Meantime it was the horse that held his eager
eye. The mule was good too, but the horse to
him was priceless—a red roan two hands taller
than any Indian pony with the straight legs that
make speed and the deep barrel that carries bottom. The horse was in splendid condition. Its
sleek coat glowed like a garnet in the sun as it
cropped the thick grass and lashed a long tail at
flies.

The white man came out of the timber on the
other side of the canyon with an armful of wood.
He threw it down and stood with his rifle in his
hands looking all around him. He was a tall
young man with thick yellow hair hanging to his
shoulders and a face burned by sun and wind to
the color of a piece of meat.

Now a temptation came to Black Wolf that
made his fingers twitch. The white man was

more than a hundred paces away and that was
too far for a sure shot. Black Wolf had been
trained never to shoot at game or enemy more
than sixty paces away unless it was necessary.
Moreover, as he had read dream and sign he was
not to kill but only to steal horses.

He ought not to shoot but his fingers itched for
the bow-string. And he was a bowman of unusual
power. More than once he had put an arrow into
a deer at over a hundred paces.

If he shot and missed he had a choice between
precarious flight and a battle against a man with
a gun. But if he shot and reached heart, throat or
eye, his fortunes were made. He would have not
only the horse but also the rifle, and the yellow
hair of the white man would hang at his belt.
Ute scalps as well as Ute ponies then he would
take. He would return a warrior and a rich man
and women would dance the scalp dance in his
honor. . . .

His mind only half assenting his fingers fitted
an arrow to the string. Moving cautiously as the
white man turned his head he braced himself
against a rock and with a firm sure pull drew the
arrow. . . .

He had drawn it almost to the head when a
magpie came flitting from bush to bush and gave
its loud harsh cry as it saw him. The white man

whirled on his heel and stood studying the bushes.

Black Wolf's right arm lost its strength as though the muscle had been cut, and a feeling of guilt and fear stabbed his heart. Motionless, scarcely breathing he crouched while the magpie perched almost over him, turning its head slowly from side to side, looking at him first with one eye then with the other. He could not bear its look.

When the white man had turned again to his work Black Wolf crept silently away, the magpie flying before him.

He went back to where he had hidden his horses, made a prayer, lay down and did not move again until the stars told him it was near midnight. Then he rode to the little canyon at a point about half a mile above where the white man was camped.

A rough and difficult way led up this canyon to the top of the range.

Here he tied his horses short to the same tree with a hitch that could be released by a single jerk.

It was the first hour after midnight when he felt the wind with a wet finger and went down the canyon, placing each foot with care. . . .

CHAPTER FOURTEEN

I

HE snort of the buckskin mule tore Sam's eyes open and jerked him upright.

He had slept through louder sounds. The squall of a bobcat, the hoot of a horned owl, the snuffle and spatter of a family of black bears about the waterhole had not disturbed his rest. But he had trained his ears to listen for that warning snort even when he was asleep.

He was wide awake now, hoping it was only another lion that had scared his animals. Next minute he was up, rifle in hand and running toward where he had picketed them.

Ropes cut with a sharp knife told him the story. He stood still a moment and way up the canyon heard shod hooves striking rock. . . .

He ripped out a few curses but he wasted no time at all. He knew what his chances were without any long thinking. If the Indians were many it was a case of dead loss. If one or two had done the trick he might yet get his stock back.

They didn't know he had waked up. They would figure on him not to start till daylight. He knew they had gone up the canyon by the sound he had heard and there he had another bulge on them. Otherwise he would have had to wait till daylight to look for tracks. Up the canyon they would have to go as far as the top of the range.

They would ride all night and camp at daybreak, for a grass-fed horse cannot go many hours at a stretch and needs an hour on the best of grass for every two hours he travels. He knew a meat-fed man can run down a grass-fed horse if he has anything like an even break.

Working fast and silently he rolled his possibles in his buffalo robe and cached it in the fork of a tree far back in the timber. He carried nothing but a few pounds of dried meat and his rifle.

Four dark hours he stumbled up the little canyon which narrowed to a gulch with a thin trickle of water in the rocky stream-bed. Round pebbles rolled under his fumbling feet and more than once threw him to his knees. Thick brush lashed at his face and he butted through it with his eyes closed.

This was a little-travelled trail made mostly by game crossing from one side of the range to the other.

Now and then he came to a shallow pool and took a quick drink for he was hot and sweating. Whenever he drank he ate jerked meat, tearing the tough strips with his teeth as he strode along. Often he heard the smash of brush and the thump-thump of a running deer. Fire-eyes of night hunting animals stared and vanished. Owls hooted and foxes barked.

Just before daylight he came to the edge of an open and lay down to wait till he could see. This far he knew the Indians must have followed the same route. Here he must pick up the trail.

Dawn showed him one of the wide grassy swales that lie just below timberline with short dense forest of dark spruce all around it and purple flowers patching forty acres of thick grass. An angular peak of bare rock was outlined against the paling sky beyond.

Here they might have stopped but he didn't think so. Over the divide and down into the first canyon on the other side they would almost certainly go to camp for they would be harder to find in the broken country of the western slope.

Snow patches on the peak showed red in the rising light and the swale shone with a million sun-touched dewdrops.

He skirted the open keeping just inside the

timber. His eyes were glued to the ground except when he stopped for a long careful look all around.

He felt new strength in his legs when he found fresh tracks where three horses and a mule had crossed the open and gone up toward the crest of the range. Only one horse was ridden. He could tell that by the way it wrangled the other three.

It was a solitary warrior he had to deal with. He pulled up his belt, ate a chunk of meat, drank at the last pool of snow water and took the plain trail at a fast clip, watching it forty feet ahead, never wavering for direction.

When the sun was an hour high he was crossing the top of the divide where grass grew short and thick as fur on a fox and low arctic willow patched the slopes and ground-pine crouched and writhed in an endless battle with a never-resting wind. An eagle patrolled a rocky spur to the north and from a ledge a great mountain ram with curling horns looked down at him and gave a long whistling snort of surprise.

He crossed the divide and looked down upon a canyon which carried glimpses of shining water through forest of pine and spruce and aspen toward the far-away shadowy gorge of the Rio Grande.

Somewhere in that timbered canyon the Indian

had hidden for the day and was watching his back track while the horses fed.

Sam left the tracks as soon as he saw they led down into the canyon, swung a mile to the west and took to the first timber on top of the ridge that bounded the canyon on that side. Slowly he worked his way down, first through dense dark spruce forest where the ground was littered with white fallen trunks like the rotting bones of dead monsters and sun came through only in patches, then into the lower forest of pine and fir shooting up a hundred feet in clean straight stems, opening into glades edged with the white and green of young aspen. Broods of grouse here ran like chickens from his path and deer that had never seen a man trotted aside and turned to stare at him with shy curiosity.

Keeping his course by the slope and the look of the timber, he never rested till he peered out from the forest across the open bottom of a canyon with a willow-bowered stream in the middle of it. Creeping out to this cover he made his cautious way to the first place a mounted man would have to ford, and saw where his quarry had crossed.

On down the creek, often in icy water to his waist, he made his way until he found a ford where nothing had crossed. Then he knew the

Indian was hidden somewhere in the dense forest on the slope above. He climbed the opposite hill a little way and hid where he had a long look up and down.

It was a crafty man he was trailing. Indians that had stolen horses generally made one long hard run and then went into camp, feeling safe because they had left their enemies afoot. They were cunning enough but they lacked the long patient care that keeps a good mountain man safe, just as they lacked his power of quick and sure decision.

Sam would not have been surprised to see his horse grazing in the open and to spot the Indian near by, but he had no such luck. This wary buck must have taken the horses far up the mountainside to some hidden glade and there he would keep them till near dark. Sooner or later he would have to come out. He would take the trail again. Sam waited for him, grim and motionless, with cramped legs and gnawing belly—for he had eaten the last of his meat.

2

The sun was down but the light still good when he heard the unmistakable sound of steel striking rock way up the canyon. He could feel himself gather and harden, gut and muscle. He looked into his priming pan and cocked his rifle.

After a little while he could hear the steady drum and shuffle of hooves in the trail but presently the sound stopped. He knew the Indian must have left the horses behind and gone ahead to scout. . . . This was a crafty buck for fair. . . . Sam moved no more than a rock while he knew the Indian was studying the trail from somewhere within a hundred yards or so.

Hooves moved again. They splashed in the last ford he had studied and out of the willow brush along the creek came his own buckskin mule, tied short neck and neck with a spotted Indian pony. Ten feet behind the span the Indian rode out of the brush, sitting Sam's roan, watching ahead with a steady anxious eye, leading another horse.

Sam saw him over a rifle sight that drew slowly, steadily toward a bead.

The buckskin mule, catching a familiar whiff on the wind, suddenly planted both forefeet, bringing the spotted pony up short, cocked his ears forward and gave a long snort of amazement.

The Indian, quick as a scared prairie-dog, dropped behind the roan, showing only one leg and a hand clutching the mane. At the same time he gave a yell and a kick and the roan sprang into a run, knocking the mule and pony out of the way, thundering down the trail.

There was nothing for it. . . . Rising to his feet Sam covered his own good horse and pulled the trigger.

The crash of his rifle filled the canyon. The roan made a last mighty plunge, stuck his nose into the dirt and somersaulted like a shot rabbit, spilling his rider ten feet ahead.

The fallen man rolled over twice and came up on his feet, facing Sam, who stood coolly pouring out a measure of powder to reload.

Now would the Indian take to the brush at once or try to get in an arrow first? He did neither. Deliberately he thumped himself on the chest with his fist and gave his battle yell. "Eeough . . . yough . . . yough!" Then he snatched a knife from his belt and dashed at Sam, running straight for his death as though he craved it.

So fast he ran that Sam had no time to prime his pan. He dropped the rifle, drew his long Green River knife and crouched to meet the charge.

The Indian sprang hard and sudden. They both missed with their knives and rolled down the hill, locked hard in each other's arms and struggling to see which should first get a hand loose for action.

Sam felt steel bite his back and jerked himself free as they bumped a little spruce. He came to his knees and the Indian rose above him with blood on his knife and blood in his eye. Sam saw an opening and took a long chance, throwing his heavy knife with an overhand jerk he had learned from the Mexicans. It buried almost to the hilt in the brown naked belly of his foe, and the Indian pitched down upon him, his hands closing in a hard spasm on Sam's throat.

A minute he writhed, choking, his eyes full of red as though he were drowning at the bottom of a sea of blood. Then the Indian's grip broke, Sam threw him off and they lay a few feet apart, gasping, neither able to move.

After a long moment the Indian rolled over and came up on an elbow and Sam also half rose to meet him, feeling as though his head was a ball of iron he could scarcely move.

The Indian's lifted hand said feebly in sign language that he was dying and Sam was glad to let him die in peace.

They lay there like picnickers on the grass, their battle fury spent with their blood. Antagonists by accident they looked at each other without hatred, with a mild surprise.

In a thin husky voice the Indian began to chant

his death song. Three times he started and each time his voice died in a gurgle. Then his throat began to swell and turn purple for the knife had pierced his lung. Suddenly a great gout of purple blood broke from his mouth and he fell on his back, twitched his knees, quivered all over and died with a long deep rattling sigh.

Sam lay still, feeling his strength come back slowly, while the peace of evening crept down the canyon. A vesper sparrow sang and trout began leaping for gnats in a smooth pool, breaking its polished surface with arcs and circles of silver.

When at last his breath came easy he crawled down to the creek and drank and rested and drank again. He felt of his back and found a long shallow cut under one shoulder blade and knew that he would lose enough blood to weaken him but that he wasn't rubbed out.

Slowly he got to his feet, found his legs sound, straightened up and took a deep breath.

Weak he stood, but proud, alone and little but sufficient to his fate—a blood-stained atom of unconquerable life.

CHAPTER FIFTEEN

I

F OR the third time Sam Lash came to the door of the padre's house. Once he had come as a hungry waif to be fed and once as a man triumphant and bearing gifts.

This time he came sore, dirty and half starved, his buckskin stained with blood and his shoulder swollen so that he could scarcely move his arm.

Apple trees heavy with fruit hung branches over the high wall behind the padre's house. From within came the voice of a woman singing at her work and bees in the garden accompanied her with a deep sleepy hum. The padre's house seemed rooted in permanence and blessed with peace.

Sam knocked at the door and waited. After a while a girl opened it. She was a pretty brown girl of seventeen—one of the padre's many "nieces." The padre always had pretty nieces in his house.

The girl's eyes widened in fear as she stared at Sam Lash, making him think for the first time in many days how he must look, unshaven, dirty and haggard. She nodded and closed the door quickly in his face when he asked for the padre.

Her master greeted Sam with a suave smile that revealed no surprise.

"How are you, friend?" he asked in his rich voice of a priest, in his carefully learned, heavily accented English. "Come in!"

He led Sam into a long cool room, white-walled, dim-lit by two narrow barred windows set with talc. The room contained only a bed rolled and covered with a Navajo blanket, making a low comfortable seat, a heavy wooden table and a chair, both homemade of yellow pine. In a corner was a canopied shrine where a wooden Christ obscurely writhed on his cross and on the wall hung bright pictures of saints with folded hands and rapt faces.

"Sit down, friend!" the priest commanded.

Sam sat on the bed, resting his good shoulder carefully against the wall and the padre perched on the chair sideways, erect, looking at him with alert shrewd eyes that shone with something like triumph.

"What brings you here, my son?" he asked.

"And what can I do to serve you. . . . My house is yours. . . ."

Sam Lash moved and winced a little. His mood was truculent.

"I reckon you know what brings me here," he said. "I reckon you know all about it. . . . When I got back to Bent's they told me old Salazar had come with about ten of his sheep-herders and taken Lola away. Nobody there felt any call to try and stop him. . . . They told me she hollered and carried on. . . . And jest as I was leaving that evil-eyed old wench Louisa told me to come to you. That was all she told me—that was all I could get out of her. . . ."

The padre heard this without a flicker.

"What hurts your shoulder, my son?" he enquired.

"I rubbed out a Cheyenne that tried to leave me afoot," Sam explained, "and he put a knife in my humpribs. . . . I killed my own horse in the ruction. And then I got caught in the damnedest storm that ever broke, and lost another horse in that and caught the ague in this cut. . . . I've had every kind of hard luck this side of hell!"

It was half a complaint and half a boast.

"I've still got my hair," he added grimly,

"and that's about all I have got that I started with. . . ."

The padre nodded in grave sympathy. Sitting safe in his house he sympathized remotely with the wandering victim of storm and battle.

"Have you eaten, son?" he enquired softly.

"Not since yesterday," said Sam Lash. "But that ain't nothing. . . . What I want to know. . . ."

"Wait!" The padre held up a hand. He rose and walked rapidly out of the room. His commanding voice in a far part of the house came back faintly and obedient lazy voices answered it.

Sam sat uneasy for a long while. Then came in a little old bearded shrivelled greaser in a ragged shirt and leather pants, barefooted. He motioned Sam to come along and Sam followed him across the *placita* and into another room at the back corner of the house. There was nothing in it but a large wooden tub full of steaming water and a pile of clothes on a blanket.

The little old man told Sam to sit down and started to pull off his moccasins. It was the first time he could remember that anybody had ever done that for him but he was so stiff in the back he let the greaser have his own way. When it came to getting his shirt off he needed help because it was plastered to his back with dry blood.

The little man soaked it off with hot water so it hardly hurt at all. He shaved Sam and washed him as if he had been a baby. Then he doused the wound with some kind of medicine and rubbed it with grease. When he had dried and combed him he handed Sam clothes—first a linen undershirt and a pair of long linen drawers and Missouri wool socks, then a blue shirt and a pair of black leather pants split and laced Mexican fashion from the knee down.

Sam walked out of there feeling weaker, feeling softened like a piece of tough rawhide that a squaw dips in water and works and dresses with gentle hands.

The little man then led him to another room where the padre waited for him and greeted him kindly.

Sam could hardly see the padre. He could see nothing but the table which shone under the light of two thick white candles. It was spread with a white cloth and set with hammered silver dishes rubbed bright as a new blade. In the middle of the table stood a great bowl filled with a stew and it reached across the room and touched his nose with its savory steam of young mutton, brown beans and chile, making him slaver so he had to swallow, waking the hunger that had died of neglect under his tightened belt.

[195]

When they had sat down a red-skirted, soft-footed girl came in and set before each a good-sized gourd filled with liquor. The padre lifted his with grace, with a smile.

"This brandy was made from grape wine by the Brothers in El Paso forty years ago next fall," he said. "I hope you will like it. . . . I drink to your good health!"

To the last drop the ancient brandy slid down Sam's throat, gentle as spring water, leaving no such trail of fire as the corn liquors he had mostly known. And yet in a minute he could feel it to his fingers and his toes, flooding him with a weakening happiness.

He sat grinning like a possum, feeling a helpless fool. The grim determinations he had brought here were still in his mind, but the grim mood that supported them was dissolving. . . . Warm water, brandy and kindness were breaking a strength that knew how to feed only on battle.

Now the girl was filling a deep silver plate with the stew and putting beside it another piled high with corn cakes, steaming hot and thin as the blade of a knife. In place of the brandy gourd stood a cup of red wine that he could never empty.

He ate with the silent ferocity of a famished

animal, crouching red-faced over his plate. Too many desperate hungers he had known ever to eat with lazy grace like the padre, who plucked choice morsels from the stew with long clean finger nails, plumped them neatly into his mouth and licked his fingers clean before he lifted his wine cup.

At first Sam's hunger seemed to grow as he ate and he looked uneasily at the dwindling stew and followed the girl with anxious eyes when she carried it away. But she was soon back with a large boiled fowl almost buried under potatoes and carrots. She brought him more tortillas and filled his cup.

When the chicken was a wreck of bones she came with a plate of custard cooked with raisins and *pinones* and a cup of black coffee, and when he had got outside of that Sam knew that at last, and for the first time in days, he was full. He sank back in his chair, flushed and covered all over with a fine dew of sweat. . . . He became aware of the padre's tolerant smile.

In the padre's eyes shone a light of native good fellowship strong enough to overcome a prejudice, but in them also was the serpent wisdom of the ancient church to whom all men are one to be saved and all are children to be ruled.

"Did you enjoy your supper, my son?" he asked.

Sam nodded his solid satisfaction.

"Muchas gracias!" he said. "That was the one best feed ever I et."

Sam filled a pipe and the padre rolled native tobacco in a corn husk. He clapped his hands and a girl came running with a coal. They lit and puffed, each waiting for the other to begin.

The padre was a subtle man, but Sam was not.

"What I want to know," he blurted at last, "is what SHE said. Does she want me back? Because if she does . . ."

The padre raised a hand, deprecating such brutal gringo directness.

"She has suffered much," he evaded. "She came to me, her Father in God, for comfort. She has been much in my house ever since she returned to Taos. I counselled forgiveness. . . ."

"What were they going to do with her?" Sam demanded.

"They wanted to send her to a convent in Durango," the padre replied after a moment of consideration.

"And she wouldn't go?"

The padre waved aside the question of her choice as irrelevant.

"I told them not to," he said. "She has no vocation and besides she will probably have a baby."

Sam meditated this over slow puffs.

"What else did you tell 'em, padre?" he asked at last.

The padre knocked yellow ash off his cigarette and stared at its glowing tip a full minute before he spoke.

"I told them to forgive," he said at last. "I told them you are a brave strong young man who any might be proud to have for a son. I said, when this strong brave young man returns—and he will return—let us receive him. I said, the arms of the church are open to all who have faith, and God's will must be ours. I said, let us receive this man into the church and then into the family. I said, let him be married again in the rite of the church and become one of us and he will strengthen us against our enemies."

Sam sat silent, grappling with smooth words.

He had come for a woman determined to take her by stealth or force as he could. He had come ready to fight.

He had come for a woman and he was being offered a church and a family.

How many strings were tied to this woman? She was anchored like a trap by hidden chains. . . .

What was a church to him? . . . He remembered Christmas in Kentucky and his father reading with slow words and pointing finger from the

family Bible and the story about the babe in the
manger and a tall itinerant preacher yellow with
malaria shouting about hell fire, making women
cry and carry on. . . . He remembered adobe
churches in little Mexican towns, bells ringing
lazy mellow dingdongs, priests droning strange
words, dressed up greasers going to early mass
and coming out to spend the day pulling chickens,
dancing and drinking red wine. . . . He remembered *penitentes* in Passion Week lashing bare
bloody backs, toting a great cross up a hill to nail
a man upon it. . . .

All of these things were church. . . . And her
breasts were white and round and once incredibly
a long time ago they had pillowed him. . . .

The padre, watching him close, thrust again
with smooth quick words.

"The Salazars, you know, have a grant of
land from the government across the mountains
on the Cimarron. They are supposed to send men
there, build and plant, make a new outpost against
the Indians and the Texans, trade with the Sioux,
the Cheyenne and the Rapaho. But who is to
lead? They need a man who knows Indian language and how to fight Indians. . . . I said to
old Salazar, here God has sent you a son who
can do what the sons of your loins cannot. And
he listened to me patiently for he is always dis-

gusted with his own sons. They spend their nights with women and their days betting on cockfights. . . . I said here is a man who has trapped and fought all over the mountains. And he knows that the days of the trapper are soon over. Already beaver is worth half what it was and the best of the streams have all been exhausted. This man I said is able to do what you need of a son. He will settle your lands and make the title good in your family. He will become a Mexican citizen. . . .

Sam lifted an interrupting hand. He was getting too much all at once. . . . He had come for a woman. He was being offered a church and a ranch and a nation. He was to plow and build and trade. . . . All of these things, it seemed, went with the woman as the tail goes with the hide. Everything that binds a man down goes with a woman. What a hell of a lot of things are tied to a skirt!

The valley of the Cimarron where he had been a week ago. . . . Soil that would cut black under a plow, water that would turn a mill, grass for a thousand cows. . . . He sprawled in the sun and watched two birds flutter and couple. . . .

Timber and stone to build a house . . . a thickwalled house to shelter his homeless spirit, a house that would hold him like a trap. . . .

Her hold soft but unbreakable about his shoulders, her tangled hair, the cleave and grip of her body that had held him, go where he would. . . .

He could not get these things straight.

Think what he would he always thought back to her.

Go where he will a man comes back to a woman. She pulls him down, she holds him down. . . . She sucks out of him power and longing to go.

She makes him plow and build who would rather wander and fight. . . .

For a long time he sat silent trying to think, trying to frame a reply, but no words came. He could not match the words of the priest. . . . He could not refuse.

"What do you want me to say, padre?" he asked at last, helplessly.

The padre moved back his chair and stood. His head was lifted and his face was solemn.

"You must give me your word that you will be married in the rites of the church. . . . You must become one of us. . . ."

Sam got up and held out his hand.

"There it is," he said. "And I ain't never gone back on it yit."

The padre shook hands with him warmly.

"Come," he said and Sam followed him out into the hallway that pierced the front of the house and across the *placita* to the door of another room. The padre opened the door on absolute darkness. He clapped his hands and the girl who had waited on them came with a candle. The padre took it as he entered and went about touching the tips of other candles in tall silver holders that stood on the floor, bringing to light a small square windowless room hung from floor to ceiling with some black stuff. At the far side of it was a shrine under a life sized figure of Christ crucified with crimson blood vividly painted on his yellowing waxen limbs and his thorn-bitten brow. The room smelled heavily of incense. It was hard to breathe in there.

Sam stood uneasily sweat prickling out all over him. The black walls and heavy air made him feel trapped and the ghastly symbol of man's eternal agony was to him nothing but the image of a corpse.

The padre, with his eyes fixed on the sacred figure, with a solemn face like a Crow medicine man in a sweat lodge, went down upon his knees. He bent his head, murmuring. His groping hand found Sam's. Gently, insistently, he tugged. . . .

Sam hesitated, he wavered, he felt like breaking for the door. But his knees gave, as so much in him had given and he knelt. . . . Beaten he knelt before the God of her people.

He bent his head and closed his eyes mainly to shut out the figure on the wall for to him it was only a reminder of death, but it was printed on his retina. He could not escape it. . . . Slowly it changed. The lean and broken body seemed to fill and bloom like a ripening fruit, the yellowed skin softened and glowed with the tints of young and living flesh, the wounded torso swelled into curving splendor. . . . The image of his desire ousted Christ from his cross and walked smiling to meet him.

He got to his feet in a daze and met the padre's look with a smile of bewildered peace. The padre seized his hand, looked long into his eyes—then with a sudden grip almost crushed his fingers.

"My son, my son!" His suavity was gone. His voice almost broke. "You have come to your God!"

They went back across the *placita,* the padre lighting the way with his candle.

"Now you must rest," he said.

"But padre, ain't there no way you could get word to her now? How long will it take to make this deal?"

The padre walked on rapidly.

"Patience, my son," he said. "These things take time. . . ."

At last he stopped before a door and stood,

his face yellow in the glare of his candle, smiling.

"This is my room for honored guests," he said formally, his hand on the latch. "Often my parishioners come to me when they are in bitter trouble and this room I have set apart for them. Many a beautiful girl, crossed in love and at war with her family, has found the peace of God here and has slept in this room. It is perfumed with the presence of beautiful souls. I hope you will sleep well. . . ."

Words, beautiful words. . . . Sam groped for words of answer. But the padre had pushed the door ajar and placed the candle in his hand.

"Good night, my son," he said and padded swiftly away.

Sam looked after him a moment and then pushed open the door, holding his candle high.

The light of it was reflected in her eyes as she stood waiting for him at the far side of the room.

Sam rocked on his heels in the shock of surprise for he had not caught the padre's hint.

Her heavy hair hung loose about her shoulders. Her eyes seemed to have grown because her face was thinner.

Her face was a record of all she had felt. He was not the only one who had lived through storms and battles.

[205]

Her head was high and her look was proud. She seemed about a foot taller than he remembered and there was no welcome in her eyes or on her lips. She seemed tall and terrible and Sam felt as though he were shrinking every minute.

Just as before, it was his weakness that softened her. After all, she had won. . . . Tenderly triumphant she smiled, looking down, but did not move. He must come to her—he who had run away.

He touched her at first as though she had been of dangerous substance but when his hands felt her unresisting warmth he lost his fear. He crushed her in his arms, and her face, backflung to meet his mouth, was a mask of willing pain.

Antagonists who could neither triumph, they struggled in a grip neither could break. . . .